THE MOON BAMBOO

THE MOON BAMBOO

THICH NHAT HANH

Translated from the Vietnamese
by Vo-Dinh Mai and Mobi Ho

Illustrations by Vo-Dinh Mai
Introduction by Mobi Ho

Parallax Press
Berkeley, California

Parallax Press
P.O. Box 7355
Berkeley, California 94707

ISBN 0-938077-20-1

"The Moon Bamboo" and "A Lone Pink Fish" were translated by Mobi Ho;" "The Stone Boy" and "Peony Blossoms" were translated by Vo-Dinh Mai; with assistance
from Therese Fitzgerald, Arnold Kotler, Annabel Laity,
and Elin Sand. Cover design by Gay Reineck. Back cover
photograph by Cao Ngoc Phuong. Composed in 10 point
Bookman on Macintosh SE by Parallax Press.

Contents

Translator's Introduction

As a storyteller, I am often asked by children, "Is the story true? Did it really happen?" I usually turn the question back to the children, "That is the way the story has been told for a long time. What do you think?" I want them to hold the story in their own hearts and discover what is true for themselves. To my way of thinking, all stories that are told from the heart, that arise from one person's experience or an entire people's experience, are indeed true. Truth is experienced and related in many different forms, from many different perspectives. There is conventional seeing and then the seeing that arises from the hidden depths of our being.

The stories in this collection are an unusual blending of these two different ways of seeing. Much of the content is based on actual persons, conversations, and events, but Thich Nhat Hanh uses these as points of departure into a world filled with miracles and wonders—a world in which a mountain manifests as a boy, a girl becomes a pink fish, a woman divides herself in two. Many of us consider this the realm of children's fairy tales, and we might initially be surprised that Thây (the form of address for Buddhist monks in Vietnam, meaning "teacher") intends these stories every bit as much for adults as for children. I am reminded of his Dharma talks in which, for the first twenty minutes or so, he speaks to the children, but he

also speaks to the adults through them. This draws
the adults into the greater understanding that be-
gins when we allow ourselves to see with the joyful
ease of a child.

Through this passage into what is normally
considered magical, we discover that we have been
led back to the miraculousness of daily life itself—
the familiar sound of a mother calling her daughter to wash her feet before the evening meal, the
taste of a slightly unripe guava fruit, holding a
child's hand while strolling leisurely through a
shaded garden. These are miracles too. Indeed, as
Thây enjoys saying, "The real miracle is not to
walk on water, but to walk on earth."

Along with the universal wisdom Thich Nhat Hanh
embodies and expresses in all his writing and
teaching, these stories share with us the deep experience of Vietnam—the spirit of the Vietnamese
earth and sky and people, as well as the unbearable
suffering of its recent history. Thich Nhat Hanh's
voice cannot be separated from the voice of his
people: "An artist, by expressing his own hopes and
pains, can speak for a nation, because the artist's
sentiments are so deeply resonant with those of his
people." These stories emerge from Thich Nhat
Hanh's experience of war, exodus, and living in exile, and evoke the images and emblems of Vietnamese myth.

The golden bird and the old man beneath the
sea in "The Stone Boy" remind us of the primordial imagery of Vietnam's creation story. The
Mother of Vietnam was the heavenly goddess Au
Co, who transformed herself into a white bird in

order to visit the young planet Earth. But when she swallowed a handful of fragrant soil, she lost her power to return home to the 36th heaven, and the tears she shed in loneliness became the nurturing rivers of Vietnam. Happily, Au Co met a Sea Dragon Prince, and together they parented the first one hundred Vietnamese. The Vietnamese soul is imbued with both the contemplative spirit of high mountain peaks reaching towards Au Co's heavenly home and the turbulent, vital activity of the sea. Often, in Vietnamese stories, tears of suffering become the refreshing streams of healing and reconnection to the homeland, to the Mother.

Blending fiction and non-fiction, imaginary characters in Thich Nhat Hanh's stories weave through the lives and experiences of actual persons. In "The Stone Boy," accounts of attacks on villages, conditions in prison camps, and the plight of children wandering in search of their parents are based on actual events Thây witnessed or was told firsthand.

Vietnamese readers will recognize a number of actual persons encountered in this story. The eccentric Taoist monk, for instance, is based on the well known "Coconut monk," so named because he is said to have eaten little more than coconuts. When I lived with the Vietnamese Buddhist Peace Delegation in Paris (headed by Thich Nhat Hanh) from 1973 to 1976, my friend Chi Huong told me about the Coconut monk. I learned how he kept a cat and mice who lived in harmony, and how he had a great bell cast from war shrapnel. I saw a photograph of the island where he and his followers lived, their long hair tied in knots upon their heads, their large mural of Jesus and Buddha shaking hands. Reading "The Stone Boy," we find it quite natural for the protagonist, who has spent thousands of moons listening to the songs of wind, birds, and trees, to befriend the Coconut monk.

During Stone Boy's incarceration, we are introduced to the 300 Buddhist monks held at Chi Hoa Prison for their refusal to be drafted. The fast of these monks began on March 2, 1974. I remember clearly the Delegation receiving a letter they had written, which was smuggled out of prison. Three days after the fast began, 142 more monks were arrested. In response to international protest, the government of South Vietnam claimed that the fasting prisoners were not monks but draft dodgers who had only shaved their heads and put on monastic robes. The fast continued for a month, and ended only when the monks were scattered to various prisons, effectively cutting off all outside contact. I am glad Stone Boy helps us remember the witness of these monks.

"A Lone Pink Fish" also weaves fact and fiction into a deeper truth. In the late 1970s, Thich Nhat Hanh and several close associates were involved in a project to rescue and assist Vietnamese boat people adrift at sea, with nowhere to land. I spent several weeks with this group aboard a hired ship in the South China Sea. We were looking for refugee boats, many of which had been turned away from the shores of Thailand and Malaysia, to assist them with their basic needs and to help them find refuge.

Hong's accounts about specific boats and refugees were gathered from among accounts told by these boat people. The "Shantisuk," too, was a real boat, and I know some of those who sailed on her. Knowing that Hong's tales of rape and murder, drowning and callousness, are based on the actual experiences of enormous numbers of people increases our awareness of the urgency of the refugees' plight. Yet it is the bodhisattva Hong who remains most deeply imprinted on my heart. I know she is real, for I have seen her in the eyes of certain people I have met.

"The Moon Bamboo" and "Peony Blossoms" are stories of life in exile—separation from family, culture, and homeland. "The Moon Bamboo" reads as a timeless fairy tale, while "Peony Blossoms" is fully anchored in contemporary life. Both stories describe the journey to the awareness of "interbeing"—the interconnectedness of all life which can heal the agonies of separation. For Mia, Doan, and Tanh, exile becomes an occasion for profound realization.

The children ask, "Is the story true? Did it really happen?" On a number of occasions, Thây's characters stop for a moment, and pay attention to their breathing. Mindful of their breathing, they are able to calm and refresh themselves, restore order to difficult situations, and return to their deepest selves. When I read these passages, I find that if I, too, stop and take three slow, mindful breaths, I "become" the character, and I "become" myself as well. Are the stories true? Breathing together, we can find the answer in our own hearts.

Mobi Ho
March 1989

The Stone Boy

The Stone Boy

Tô stopped playing her bamboo flute. She could taste the bittersweet saltiness of the tears streaming down her cheeks. Resting the flute on her thigh, she lifted a corner of her peasant blouse and wiped her tears.

The forest was crisp and cool that April morning. Listening to the rustle of young, spring leaves, Tô could remember how irresistibly tender and green they had once appeared to her. But her memory of colors was already beginning to dim, just six months after she had lost her sight.

The night before, like every night for weeks, Tô had carefully, even desperately, touched her mother's face, hoping never to forget a single line. When she tried to picture her father, who had died two years before, no image came to her. Touching her flute, Tô remembered how her father, a woodcutter, had brought her this piece of bamboo and helped her make it into a musical instrument. He taught her how to rub the flute with a dry banana leaf to give it a rich color, and he taught her how to play.

Father would always walk with Tô part way to school, to the place where the road forked at the foot of Fragrant Hill. With his machete on his shoulder, he would go into the deep forest, and little Tô would walk up and down two more hills to the Upper Village School, carrying a wooden box filled with school supplies and her flute, and

swinging an ink bottle tied to her finger. Father
had made her school box from the thinnest wood
available, and it was very light to carry. After just
a few months, the wood became dark and shiny
like the flute.

Each day Tô would return from school to have
lunch with her mother. In the afternoon, her father would come home with a heavy load of wood
on his back, and after supper, she and Father
would take a leisurely walk alongside the stream
or in the forest.

On Wednesdays, the family would rise at dawn
and go to the Lower Village market, hauling the big
cart filled with firewood. By the time they reached
Upper Village, Tô's legs were already tired, and Father would stop the cart and let her sit on top of
the wood pile. When all the wood was sold, Mother
would buy rice and other essentials, and one special treat for Tô. By noon they would be back
home, and Mother would cook a pot of rice. But Tô
was never hungry on Wednesdays. Satiated by her
special treat, she asked permission to go outside
and play, and usually she walked to the edge of the
forest. Tô loved playing the flute along the bank of
the gentle stream which ran near their house, and
she loved gathering beautiful wildflowers whose
names she did not know.

Then Father died. Less than one year after joining
the army, he was killed in combat. When the news
reached home, Mother screamed uncontrollably.
Tô, only seven at the time, did not understand
what death meant. She saw her mother rolling in
the dirt, crying, and she felt torn apart inside.

Holding Mother in her arms, she understood that she would never see Father again. He was dead, just like the bird she had seen on the stream bank decomposing to become soil. Sadness entered Tô's spirit. He would not be back to play or talk with her. He would not lift her in his arms, or look deeply into her eyes again. As the days passed, Tô became sadder and sadder.

After Father's death, Tô stayed home and helped take care of the house—cooking rice, cropping and sorting vegetables and herbs—while Mother went to the forest to gather firewood. Mother's loads were smaller than Father's had been, so the family could not afford as much rice. Tô continued to take walks after supper, and she always brought her flute. She would go to the place where she and Father used to sit, and she played the short melodies he had taught her.

Sometimes while playing, Tô's sadness became so intense that she could hardly breathe. She felt as if she were in the grip of a strong vise. Breathing deeply a few times, she would refresh herself, pick up the flute again, and create songs which expressed her grief as well as her joy. As the days went by, she composed more and more tunes, and playing these made her feel better. Crying also brought a kind of relief. Tears poured from her heart, and the more she cried, the lighter her heart became.

One day while Tô was sitting in the woods deeply absorbed in playing her flute, a number of airplanes passed overhead so low they barely missed the treetops. The forest shook. Tô looked up and saw a thick, white cloud. Within seconds she felt her eyes burning and her lungs gasping for air. Choking and crying, she fell unconscious to the ground. She had no idea that the planes had spread clouds of chemical defoliants.

To's mother was horrified by the roar of the planes and the sight of the cloud above the forest. She ran out to find Tô, but it was more than an hour before she came upon the unconscious body of her daughter. Unable to revive her, she ran to the Upper Village to get a nurse. When they returned, Tô was sitting, screaming that her eyes were on fire. Both eyes were badly swollen, and she could hardly see. The nurse washed them with cotton dipped in medicine, and gave her an injection. She told Tô's mother to bring her to the district hospital, a day's travel away. But at the hospital, the doctors were not able to do anything.

When Tô visited the forest for the first time after losing her sight, it was like a dark, silent dungeon. Gradually, though, she began to notice things that she had not been aware of when she could see. In the sound of the stream, she heard an old man talking and singing. She felt the branches and leaves of the trees standing up to dance. In the sound of the wind rustling in the leaves, Tô saw thousands of hands rising into the air to wave at her. The light itself had become brighter and begun to dance. Tô came to know the sounds of thousands of friends dwelling harmoniously in the forest. From the blankets of moss, the bark of trees, and even the soil itself, creatures talked to her, telling her about their lives. Hundreds of bird songs each brought a different message. Tô responded to each one by raising her flute and playing a new and utterly beautiful melody.

Tô came to feel that Heaven had created her so that she could play the flute and communicate with the creatures of the forest. Once, a strange bird called her and she responded with a song. Tô could see the bird clearly in her mind. It had a long tail, golden feathers, and a white patch like a crown on its head. Its bright, quick eyes darted left and right. The bird sang for a while and stopped. Tô raised her flute and played in response. The bird replied with a song that communicated surprise that Tô could speak the bird's language, and pleasure to be able to sing with her. Tô played again, telling the golden bird about herself and imitating the bird's song. Delighted, Tô began to laugh, and her laughter carried through the forest like a flurry of young finches at dawn.

For nine days in a row, the golden bird came to converse with Tô's flute. Then it flew away and did not return. Tô went on playing the flute, but her heart was heavy. She would begin with soft, distant notes, as if to share her sadness with the small creatures beneath the ground. Then the sounds of her flute rose and blended with the multitude of sounds coming from the leaves and branches above. Little by little Tô forgot that she was a young girl playing an instrument, and she became a tiny creature living in the forest with thousands of friends. The sounds of the flute resonated with the cries of the other creatures. She was at one with the forest. Trees, moss, grass, and roots began to dance, and her pain dissolved. Tô was no longer only Tô. Tears streamed from her sightless eyes—warm tears like the spring sunshine, and sweet, cool tears like the pure water from the stream—and she felt a great relief.

Tô was enjoying the same warmth and lightness that she imagined the young buds felt after the cleansing rains of winter. She remembered how the defoliant chemicals had stripped the trees of their leaves. But during that winter, unusually heavy rains washed away the spray, and healthy young leaves grew back. Insects and worms were again crawling, flying, and buzzing everywhere. Just as the forest had regained its will to live, Tô had recovered her spirit.

Tô realized that someone was standing in front of her. Completely absorbed in the life of the forest, she had not heard the approaching footsteps. Someone with sweet breath and a light, gentle presence was definitely there. Tô had never before known someone with breathing so fine and pure.

"Who are you?" she asked in a shy, small voice.

There was no answer.

"Who's there? What is your name? Where are you from?" she asked again.

"Stone Boy," came the hesitant reply. "My name is Stone Boy, and I come from up the mountain."

His voice was fleeting, like a wisp of a cloud, as light as the singing of the golden bird who had visited Tô for nine straight days. Stone Boy spoke only a few words, but these were enough for Tô to envision him. He was about eleven or twelve, with delicate features in a full, oval face, like a mango.

His eyes were bright and clear. Tô liked her new friend. She pointed to the foot of the tree next to her, and invited him to sit down. "Please tell me, Stone Boy, where is your home on the mountain?"

The boy remained silent. A moment passed, and Tô spoke again. "How old are you, brother—eleven?"

"I don't know how old I am. . . . I may be very, very old. . . ."

Tô burst out laughing, and motioned him to come closer. She raised her hands and touched his face, while Stone Boy sat perfectly still and allowed Tô to explore. Yes, his face was shaped like a mango, and his skin was cool like a mountain stream in summer. His hair was long, covering most of his forehead and hanging down over his neck. When she finished, Tô laughed. "Just as I thought. You must be about eleven. Twelve, at most. Tell me where your home is and what your parents do. My name is Tô. I live with my mother nearby. My father is dead."

But Stone Boy remained silent. "He certainly is quiet," Tô thought. His being seemed made of innocence and wonder. He had said his home was up the mountain, and he obviously did not want to say anymore. "I shouldn't bother him," she said to herself, and sat down quietly next to her new friend.

Finally, Stone Boy spoke up. "Elder sister, please play your flute."

Tô laughed again. "Please don't call me elder sister. I'm only nine. Please say, 'Younger sister, play your flute for me, your elder brother Stone Boy,' and I will gladly play for you." Stone Boy repeated her words exactly, and Tô raised her flute and began to play.

Never before had Tô's flute sounded so joyous. She felt as if she were floating on a cloud amidst the sunshine and spring breezes. The entire forest floated up with her and formed an enormous cloud. Tô's flute became a large vessel carrying all of springtime. She forgot that she was blind, or that her father was dead. She had returned to her source. She was running along the hillside, her hand in Father's, and they were laughing happily. Tô heard the birds' songs falling like pearls from Heaven. She heard the loving calls of the forest, hills, and gardens—calls as familiar as Mother calling her home to wash her feet before coming in to light the lamp and sit down for supper.

Stone Boy sat still and listened. Tô knew that he must have seen the tears welling up in her eyes, and she said, "I'm crying, Stone Boy, but I am not sad. I am very, very happy."

Stone Boy asked her, "Why haven't you played such joyful tunes before? I've listened to you, and the music you play is usually so mournful."

Instead of answering his question, Tô asked, "Where were you when you heard me playing?"

"I was high up on the mountain. Every day your music reaches the top of the mountain."

"How can the sound of my flute reach the top of the mountain?"

"Oh, it can reach the clouds. I hear you every day. I heard your flute, so I came to see you. It took me two days to walk down," Stone Boy said.

"Two days? His home must be far, far up the mountain," Tô thought. She never imagined that her music could travel that far. Her flute had actually found her a new friend. Sitting next to Stone Boy, Tô did not want to move even a hair, as she was afraid to disrupt their fragile world. She did not dare talk and laugh as she would have done with her classmates at Upper Village School. She was not afraid of Stone Boy, but she felt a great respect for this quiet, but not shy, boy. He was like a clean sheet of rice paper, open and ready, and she did not want to write or draw on him without the utmost care. So they sat quietly. Then Stone Boy said, "Please tell me, younger sister, what is it like down here?"

Tô told him about her parents and her life in the little house on the hill. She told him about school, her teacher, the marketplace, and the people of Lower Village. She spoke slowly, stopping to explain words she thought he might not understand. He seemed to know very little about her life, or even her language. She explained that a "marketplace" was a large area where people gathered to buy and sell vegetables, rice, fish, and firewood. From time to time, Stone Boy asked her to stop and tell him more details. This made Tô feel like a teacher, carefully sharing her knowledge of many things.

The sun was already at noon, and Tô had to return home to prepare lunch for Mother. She invited Stone Boy to join her. Reaching out, she took his hand, and the two new friends walked out of the forest together. Even though she could not see, Tô showed Stone Boy the trees and bushes in her yard, the tools, the garden, and their small, wooden house. She only had to tell him the names of things once, and he remembered.

Tô asked Stone Boy if he was hungry, but he did not seem to understand what "hungry" or "eating" meant. This amused Tô and she laughed as she brought Stone Boy into the alcove that was used as a kitchen. Tô took out a pot, rinsed some rice, and put it on the fire. Then she went out—somewhat self-consciously, as she could feel Stone Boy watching her—to pick some garden vegetables. He helped her prepare the vegetables, and soon the meal was ready.

Stone Boy and Tô sat on the front doorstep, waiting for Mother. Stone Boy asked her how her father had been drafted into the army, and how she had been blinded by the cloud of chemicals, but their conversation stopped abruptly as Mother arrived. Tô introduced her new friend from the mountain with such thoroughness that there was nothing for him to add. Still, Mother asked him about his home and parents, but his replies were so hesitant that she concluded that Stone Boy, like thousands of other children during the murderous war, must be an orphan. So, breathing quietly to calm herself, she went to the yard and washed her hands. When she returned, she invited the children to sit down to lunch.

During the meal, Tô could tell that Stone Boy was eating very little, and that in fact he was watching her to learn how to eat. When they finished, Tô asked Mother if Stone Boy could stay. Delighted to meet such a loving, gentle boy, she agreed, and suggested that the two of them take a walk along the stream to enjoy the afternoon breeze.

As they sat on the stony bank of the stream, Tô asked Stone Boy to describe everything he saw. Hesitant at first, he soon was telling her of the blue sky, the white clouds, and the dark green forest. Tô's face shone with delight. She felt as if she could see everything through his eyes. She heard in his voice the earth itself, deep and resonant. When dusk fell, Stone Boy became silent. Tô lifted her flute and began to play. She felt herself on a rocky peak, lost in the mist, and she saw the birds, the earth, and the wind.

Mother called Tô and Stone Boy home. She lit an oil lamp and served a delicious supper of rice, lemongrass, carrots, and greens. Stone Boy was already more comfortable using his chopsticks, and chewing and swallowing. After dinner, Mother found a mat and invited Stone Boy to stay overnight. Tô was delighted. This was the first time in her life she had a friend stay in her home.

The next morning the children woke up like two young birds. Tô brought her friend into the garden and taught him hide-and-seek. They played on the grassy hillside, which was dotted with thousands of yellow and purple wildflowers. Stone Boy invited Tô to sit with him again by the brook, and he looked at the sky and the earth and told her everything he saw. Tô was happy just to sit and listen to Stone Boy—she loved his voice so—and he no longer had difficulty speaking. Tô had the impression that, not only was this a boy speaking to her, but the earth and sky were speaking to her as well.

Even after Stone Boy stopped talking, Tô continued to hear the voices of Heaven and Earth. With Stone Boy by her side, Tô was not blind.

After lunch, Mother made a brown cotton peasant shirt for Stone Boy. Imitating Tô, the boy said, "Thank you, Ma." Tô was sure that this expression pleased Mother, because she invited him to come along for their weekly market trip the next day. Tô was overjoyed, for she could explain many more new things to Stone Boy, and he could see for both of them.

In the morning, they loaded the cart with firewood. Mother stood in front with the harness over both shoulders and her hands gripping the handles. She leaned forward to pull the cart to market and noticed how much easier it was to pull than usual, as Stone Boy and Tô helped push from behind.

Tô talked all the way from Upper Village to Lower Village. She told Stone Boy to look at everything en route and asked him whether he was seeing this or that house, tree, or garden, for she knew where they were every inch of the way.

The market at Lower Village was only a small "pocket market," yet there were more than one hundred people there that day. After selling all the firewood, Mother bought rice, salt, fish sauce, and a handful of tiny live fish wrapped in a banana leaf. She also bought one orange cookie and one sweet rice cake for the two children. Then she asked them to load the cart and wait while she went to a nearby shop to buy lamp oil.

The children sat on the roots of a shady flame tree and slowly ate their sweets. Tô had barely fin-

Ished hers when the sounds of shots and screams filled the air. In an instant, the market became frantic, like a beehive burst open. Bullets whistled overhead and people threw down their belongings and ran wildly in every direction, fleeing for cover. Tô pulled Stone Boy to the ground and held her hand on the back of his head to keep him from looking up. Then the ground trembled from a huge explosion, and debris fell everywhere. Tô and Stone Boy were covered with dirt. They heard tragic, painful screams and Tô realized that a bomb had landed in the marketplace, wounding and killing many, many people. From beyond the market, gunfire blazed. Realizing that Mother might be wounded, or even killed, Tô cried out, "Oh, Ma, Ma, where are you?" Trembling, she held Stone Boy tightly to her, but Stone Boy sat up calmly and told her, "Don't worry, Ma is all right. Sit here and I will find her."

As Stone Boy stood up, bullets whizzed over his head and another terrifying explosion shook the market. Tô quickly pulled him back down, and they both lay flat in the dirt again. The second explosion was even more powerful. Blasts of hot air scorched them, and they heard buildings collapsing, dirt and debris raining down everywhere. There was a moment of stillness before the heart wrenching screams began again, but the guns were now silent.

Tô and Stone Boy lay perfectly still and listened to the crackling sounds of bamboo houses going up in flames. Stone Boy described men with guns tying the wrists of people who had no guns, and herding them off in small groups. "A lot of people are hurt," he said. "We must try to help them." Tô grasped his arm tightly. "No, not yet. We must wait until the men with guns are gone."

After a while, Stone Boy told her, "There are only wounded people in the market now," and the children made their way to a group of victims lying on the ground, moaning and crying. Villagers were trying to help with improvised bamboo stretchers. Stone Boy told Tô that many people had lost arms or hands—some had their feet crushed, while others' faces were torn apart, and small children lay in puddles of blood.

More and more people were coming out from their houses. While the villagers carried the dead and the wounded away, Tô and Stone Boy began searching for their mother. Stone Boy led Tô down to the heap of smoldering ash where the oil shop had been.

"Oh Ma, Ma, where are you, Ma?" Tô burst out crying. "Has anybody seen my mother? Please tell me if you've seen her." Several women standing nearby heard her, and shook their heads.

"They haven't seen Mother, I can tell," Stone Boy said. "They're looking for their own families. Let's go."

They walked around the market into the village. Though Tô could not see, she could feel and hear the desolation and sorrow around her. It was spring, but all was agony and despair. Each time Tô heard footsteps approach, she would ask, "Oh Uncle," or "Oh Aunt, have you seen my Ma?" Every time the reply was "No." No one had seen Mother. Mother was not among the dead or the wounded in the marketplace. Where could she be? They returned to the spot where the market had been, and an old lady said she had seen her.

"Yes, I saw your mother with a bottle in her hand," she told them. "She was leaving the oil shop, walking towards the market, when the bomb exploded."

It was the first piece of helpful information. Tô tugged on Stone Boy's sleeve, and they continued to search the neighborhood, knocking on every door and asking, "Have you seen my mother? She was carrying a bottle of oil." They left no corner or shelter untouched, but they could not find Mother.

Dusk fell, and it quickly became dark. The children were ravenous by now, so they returned to the big flame tree to find their sweet rice cake. Afterwards, they climbed up onto the cart, which was still parked where Mother had left it. The night was chilly. Though the leaves of the flame tree protected them from the heavy dew, they were cold all night. They huddled up against each other and slept on and off until morning.

As soon as Tô woke up, she knew there was a large crowd at the marketplace. Stone Boy was already awake and sitting quietly, watching her. He told her that a group of men with guns were standing around talking to the villagers. Tô surmised that the government people had come from the district headquarters. She climbed down from the cart.

"Let's go, brother Stone Boy. Let's ask them to help find Mother."

Stone Boy and Tô approached a soldier, and Tô asked him, "Sir, can you please help us find our mother?"

Stone Boy spoke up. "Sir, my little sister is blind. We came from Upper Village yesterday with our mother. She was at the market when the fighting started, and we don't know where she is now."

Stone Boy's fluency and politeness surprised Tô. The soldier did not reply. Instead, he walked over to another man and spoke with him in a low voice. The second man, in a very authoritative voice, asked them their mother's name.

"Ba Ty," Tô said. "She is a woodcutter, and our home is in the Dai Lao Forest, near Upper Village."

Tô gathered that this man was the group's commander. He turned to the villagers and asked if anyone knew anything about Mrs. Ba Ty. Someone reported that she was neither among the dead nor the wounded. Another speculated that she must have been taken away by the attackers. The commander told the children to go home and wait.

"Don't worry. If we get any news of her, we will let you know right away."

Tô and Stone Boy returned to the big flame tree to get their cart. Pushing and pulling, they managed to make their way back to Upper Village by early afternoon. Stone Boy brought Mother's purchases into the house, and Tô followed him. The little house seemed cold and empty without Mother. Tô asked Stone Boy if he was hungry, but neither of them felt like eating, so they just sat on the doorstep and stared blankly ahead of them. Neither spoke for a long time.

Then Stone Boy remembered the little fish that Mother had bought at the market, and he said, "The little fish must all be dead by now." He asked Tô to get her flute and walk with him to the stream. Though Tô had no heart to play the flute, she obliged. Stone Boy filled a bucket with water and placed all the fish in it. After a moment he spoke, "They're dead except for two survivors. One is orange, the other silver. Let's release them in the stream, Tô."

Stone Boy knelt, scooped the two little fish out of the bucket, and let them go. Tô could imagine two tiny fish happily swimming away, and her lips relaxed into a half smile. In this moment of calmness, she recalled the desperate cries of the villagers in the marketplace. Tô became agitated and overwhelmed by the images of children her own age with crushed skulls and torn limbs. She saw huge flames from the burning houses and adults lying in the dirt with their bloody insides exposed. She thought of her own mother being led away with her wrists bound together. She knew that Stone Boy must be thinking about the same things, and asked him if he thought they would ever see Mother again. Had Mother also died like a bird lying in the forest, with its head crumpled onto its chest, its feet folded under?

Tô felt enormous pressure on her chest, and it was difficult for her to breathe. She wanted to cry but instead she gasped for air like someone under water too long. The stone on which she sat was burning.

At that moment Stone Boy began to sing a strange, miraculous song. Tô had never heard anything so solemn or beautiful. It began like a thin strand of smoke rising from the thatched roof of their house as Mother cooked the evening rice. The strand of delicate sound spread out horizontally and hung suspended in the air, motionless; then it opened up like the wings of a huge, beautiful bird flying in endless, open space. The giant bird beat its wings and, high up in the sky, the wind was born and it beckoned to the clouds from the four corners of the heavens to gather around. Fire-colored, luminous clouds joined in rhythmic formations. Tô heard the whistling of pine trees swaying in the wind and the distant murmur of a fine spring drizzle descending upon the willows along the stream. She heard tiny footsteps of small children dressed in colorful clothes, holding hands, playing and singing on the grassy hillside.

The pain in Tô's chest released, and she breathed easily. The stone under her felt like a cloud. She heard the thunderous patter of wings beating in the sky, then tens of thousands of birds crying together. Suddenly, one bird flew very low, just above their heads, and delivered its song like a string of pearls stretched across the sky. Tô recognized the song as that of the golden bird who had replied to her flute music for nine days. She put her flute to her lips and played a very sad song, as sad as the purple sky at dusk, while the birds circling above listened attentively. Tô asked the birds to fly everywhere and look for her mother. The simple music cried, prayed, and begged. It flew skyward, then plummeted beseechingly to the ground. The birds scattered in every direction, and only one golden bird with a very long tail and a few small white feathers on its head remained. It sang one more short song, flitted about briefly, and then flew off towards the forest with the others.

Tô and Stone Boy sat silently for a moment. Then, she asked him, "Please tell me, who taught you how to sing like that?"

"No one. I lived for a long, long time at the top of the mountain, listening to the clouds, wind, rain, mist, and many other sounds. One day I discovered that I knew how to sing. But I only sing when the sky and the earth are ill at ease, sad, and angry, when black clouds come down towards earth and the sky is about to explode.

"And who taught you how to play your flute so beautifully? Did your mother teach you?"

"No, when Father was still alive, he taught me a few folk songs, peasant music. Like you, I listened to the voices of the trees, the wind, the stream, and the birds. But your singing is so much better! It makes me feel wonderful. It revives me. Even the birds in the forest fly down to listen to you!"

Stone Boy did not speak right away. Then he asked her, "Didn't you ask the birds to help find Mother? I am sure they heard you. They will try to do what you asked. But how can they find someone they have never seen? You and I must go ourselves and look for her."

Tô cocked her head, "How? Where? We don't have any idea where she is!"

"No, but we must look for her everywhere. Please trust me. I know we will find her. We cannot sit here forever waiting for her to come back."

Tô knew that her friend was right. They had to climb mountains and cross rivers. If one month was not enough, they had to look for two months. If one year was not enough, they had to look for two, three, or even four years. They had to find her. Tô knew that once they found Mother, everything would be all right again.

Without Mother, yesterday and today were filled with fear and worry. Once Mother was found, the gunmen would stop shooting, the children would stop being hurt, and the destruction of villages would cease. She was convinced that they had only one task—to go everywhere and look for Mother. She asked Stone Boy, "When should we start?"

"Right now. Remember the little fishes that survived and returned to the stream. They went to look for their mother. Now we must also go and find our Ma."

Tô and Stone Boy walked up the hill to their small house. Tô filled a large cotton bag with food and cooking utensils, and Stone Boy swung it over his shoulder. Tô put on the old rain jacket her father used to wear, and she hung her flute across her back. Pushing back the leaves of the front door, the two children left to find their mother.

❈   ❈   ❈

First Tô and Stone Boy went to the Upper Village. At the school gate, they asked several people if they had seen Mrs. Ba Ty, but none of them had. They walked to the Lower Village and saw soldiers standing guard in several places. Stone Boy described to Tô how there were embers and smoldering ash where houses had stood. It was a village of desolation, and people were cleaning up the terrible mess. They asked if anyone had seen their mother, but no one had. They walked around the outlying areas of the village, but still no luck, so they continued walking.

As long as the road stretched out in front of them, they walked on, not knowing where the next village might be. They climbed several hills and walked through small woods, but they did not see even one hut. It was getting dark. After crossing a bamboo bridge, they stopped for a few moments to rest their legs, cooling their feet in the stream. Tô asked Stone Boy to find three stones. She set her cooking pot on them, built a fire, and cooked some rice in the pot they brought with them.

The moon, barely a sliver, hung in the vast, dark sky. For Tô, it was no problem to eat in the dark. She and Stone Boy were famished, and they ate the whole pot of rice. Stone Boy walked to the stream and brought back water for drinking and washing, and they lay down close to one another under Father's rain jacket.

They woke up as the sun was warming the chilly air, and went down to the stream to wash their faces before setting off again to search for Mother. Tô walked close to Stone Boy, holding his arm. After crossing a thick growth, they expected to see hamlets or at least a few houses, but the dense jungle trail stretched endlessly in front of them. At nightfall, Tô proposed that they stop and make camp at a place where she heard the sound of running water. While she cooked a pot of rice, Stone Boy found a good place surrounded by trees and bushes to sleep. He broke a number of thorny branches and placed them around the spot for protection.

During the night, Tô heard the crackling of a large fire. She reached out for Stone Boy, but he was already awake, watching something. Stone Boy held Tô's hand firmly and whispered, "Keep still. There are hundreds of men with guns around a campfire near the stream. They just finished cooking rice and are about to eat it."

Tô and Stone Boy listened as the men sang strange songs with powerful rhythms which sounded like ocean waves breaking on a rocky shore. Tô sensed in their songs a force, as if they were about to stampede forward and crush everything in their way.

The group sang other songs which sounded gentler. Stone Boy watched as some men stood up and told stories, and he noticed that everyone in the group was beginning to feel more relaxed. One man, wearing green palm leaves in his hair, stood up. He held a long cane like a lance in his right hand and a flaming stick in his left. Swinging the flame in front of him, he sang:

> Our beautiful, precious land—
> I'll do my duty here.
> Three years as a soldier—
> on guard at dawn, in the office at night.
> This is my fate, so why should I complain?
>
> O, soldiers, let us cry our hearts out to the
> bamboo and wu-tung trees.
> Our suffering is like salt in an open wound.

Tô was moved by this strange, poignant song. She thought of her own father as a soldier in the jungle with scarcely enough food to eat, sleeping on hard ground, exposed to the rains, without his family to care for him when he was ill. Tô realized that these men were the same as her father. They were singing vigorously now, but soon they would be brought down by jungle illnesses, bullets, or bombs. They would lie on the ground like the little dead bird with its head twisted upon its chest, its legs and claws crumpled under its belly. This soldier's song was much closer to the ones Tô composed on her flute. It was sorrowful, and it spoke of longing and resignation. The earlier soldiers' songs were forceful, like the wind and the rain in a great storm. Tô wondered how these men could have such different voices and feelings.

When the man ended his song, there was no applause, just a long silence. One man spoke up and criticized the singer, and then the group returned to patriotic songs, infused with fight and courage. They sang for a while, and fell silent. Stone Boy and Tô could hear nothing but the occasional crackling of the big fire going out. They stayed very still and soon fell asleep.

The two children awoke to find that the strangers had gone without leaving any traces, not even ash or coal from the fire. Stone Boy and Tô started out again. They walked all day before emerging from the forest. By the time they reached a small village, night had already begun to fall. The village was surrounded by a strong, high fence of sharpened bamboo stakes, and watchtowers dotted the area. Stone Boy and Tô decided to spend the night under one of the thatched roofs of the market so that they would not have to go far to inquire about Mother in the morning.

In the middle of the night, Stone Boy and Tô woke up to the explosion of bombs. Guns blazed, and someone sounded a brass bell as an alarm. Occasionally, the gunfire became intense, and a flare burst in the sky, sending light into every corner. Bombs brought down the central roof of the market. Loose tiles and debris whizzed towards the thatched roof where Stone Boy and Tô sat. Children and adults screamed, and soldiers shouted angrily. Houses caught on fire. People ran to alert one another to put out fires in the midst of the fighting. The attackers broke through the line of defense, yelling, "Forward! Forward!" and the shooting intensified. Stone Boy kept getting up but Tô struggled to keep him down as bullets whizzed by their heads. But Stone Boy was strong and eager to help others. Tô lay trembling like a small, frightened bird. Houses were burning, people were dying, and men on opposing sides were on a murderous rampage. Before Tô knew it, the words "Ma! Ma!" escaped from her lips. Then, without fear of being hit by a bullet, she sat up and screamed at the top of her lungs.

When Tô stopped screaming, she could not believe her ears—Stone Boy was singing. He had gone into the open marketplace and started singing. She shouted, "Lie down, Stone Boy, please!" But he did not hear her. His voice rang louder and louder, and Tô heard the wind rise and flutter. The sound of the forest far away blended in with his voice. Stone Boy stood fearlessly, as if he were on a tranquil hillside. Tô felt all her sorrow and fear melt, and she began to accompany him on her flute. The sound of wings beating signalled to her that the birds had come again and were circling above.

The battle subsided. The shooting became less intense, and the screams and shouts quieted. The sound of Tô's flute rose up, and wept over the fate of the woodcutters forced to become soldiers, who never came back from the war. Her music mourned for the firewood-sellers who lost their children during a battle; for small boys and girls who wandered homeless; for soldiers who died in utter loneliness in remote mountain passes; for old women and babies who had been hit by stray bullets and bled to death unattended. Heaven and Earth heard these cries, and all the birds in the forest listened. Children and grown-ups, and even the soldiers who had just been shooting each other, were now holding their guns down and listening. Tô was begging for help from Heaven, from Earth, and from all living creatures. As her music quieted, Stone Boy's voice rose again. In his voice there was a deep faith in the interconnectedness and love among all beings which soothed all pains like a spring breeze. It was autumn dew cooling the fire of hatred, the miraculous water that brought forth young buds on dying trees.

The guns were silent now. Even the wind had quieted. The birds were flying away. Tô and Stone Boy held hands in silence. In the east, there was a hint of dawn.

Life returned slowly to the village. Several men appeared with torches blazing in the thick, white mist. People called out to their loved ones. The dead were being carted away. Rebuilding had already started. Reinforcement for the next attack was being planned, and a request for help was put through to the District Headquarters.

A detachment of men on patrol saw Stone Boy and Tô and, since they were unknown to the local people, they were arrested. A few military and civilian men suspected they were enemy scouts and threatened to shoot them on the spot. Stone Boy looked deeply at them, bewildered. He did not know what those words—scouts, couriers, spies—meant. But Tô was terrified. She burst out crying and proceeded to tell the men everything that had happened. The men did not believe her, but rather than having them shot, the Commander ordered that they be brought to the District Headquarters and turned over to the civilian authorities.

At noon, army trucks took them to the police station of the district's capital. They were given some food and nothing but a blanket and a straw mat to spend the night. Three days went by until they were taken to the provincial capital and placed in the Center for Juvenile Reform.

The Center was a large tract of land dotted with long, low buildings, and surrounded by high walls studded with glass shards. Stone Boy and Tô were brought to a room with an interrogator and a typist. Tô said right away that she was Hoang Thi Tô, nine years old, in the fifth grade, and daughter of Mr. and Mrs. Ty, woodcutters from Upper Village, An Lac District. She said that Stone Boy was her brother, twelve years old, but he was not going to any school, for he had to stay home and help their widowed mother. Then she declared proudly that their father had given his life to his country.

The interrogator asked Stone Boy to tell him all he knew about the attack at Phuoc Binh four days ago, and, yes, to tell him honestly whether he was working for the rebels. Stone Boy did exactly as he was asked, relating all the details of their search to find their mother, leading up to their arrest. When Stone Boy told the interrogator about the men with guns on the bank of the stream, Tô could sense the interrogator's suspicion. Indeed, he sat silently for a long moment and then ordered Stone Boy to be taken to Camp A and Tô to Camp D. The tall, thin secretary took Tô's hand and told Stone Boy to follow them. Though they were to be kept in separate camps, she said, they could see one another twice a day, after lunch and after supper. She added that they could ask for permission to visit at other times as well.

Although Tô was allowed to participate in all activities at Camp D's school, she could not see what was written on the blackboard, nor read the books. When it came to things that did not require eyesight, however, she did fine. After only five days, she was able to make her way around the Reform Center without a guide. And her roommate Lê, though a sharp and tough girl, liked her very much.

Stone Boy could not keep up in his school. He asked for permission to go to Tô's class and sit next to her. After mealtimes, she would teach him the basics of reading, and in less than a week, he was able to read and write simple sentences. Then

Tô showed him arithmetic, and in just one day, he learned addition, subtraction, multiplication, and division.

Most of the children at the Center were friendly, except for a few tough ones whose joy came from bullying and beating up others. Even Stone Boy was roughed up once by two older boys because he smiled when they tried to intimidate him. Though his face was bloodied, Stone Boy did not fight back. Tô happened to be there, and she ran to get help. When the authorities arrived, Stone Boy had collapsed onto the dirt floor and was bleeding profusely. He was taken to the infirmary and Tô asked for permission to sit with him. From that day on, the others began to call Stone Boy "the dumb one," because he did not fight back when he was being beaten. And Tô, of course, was called "the blind one."

By the end of that year, Stone Boy was released from the Reform Center and placed in the School for Wards of the State because of his exemplary conduct and excellent schoolwork. Tô was transferred to the School for the Blind at Bien Hoa. They were in a panic when they were told of their new destinations. They both thought that, once separated, they would never be able to find Mother. But the decision had been made. They would be allowed to correspond, and once in a while Stone Boy would be permitted to visit Tô at the School for the Blind.

❋   ❋   ❋

One night, Tô was awakened by gunshots in the distance, and she was filled with sorrow. She had just dreamed that Stone Boy was back, and they were walking side by side. It was now more than six months since she had heard from him. She had lost him in the same way that she had lost her Ma.

While Stone Boy was a ward of the state, Tô received four letters from him which she kept in a tin can among her clothes. Once in a while, she would ask a young woman who worked at the school to read them for her. As soon as his letters stopped coming, Tô asked the school's administration to make inquiries about him. They reported that Stone Boy had been transferred to the Reform Center at Vung Tau because of misconduct.

Tô could not believe that Stone Boy would do anything wrong. She had never known anyone kinder or gentler. But he was never afraid of anyone, not even those in power. Perhaps if she had been with him, this would not have happened, she thought. How could a little blind girl ever find the two persons dearest to her in the world?

During the first few months at the School for the Blind, Tô learned to read Braille. As her fingers moved along the stiff sheets of paper with dots of varying depths, images materialized in her mind, and a smile came to her lips. It was a pity there were not many of these books available. She learned to write these types of letters with both an inkless stylus and a Braille typewriter.

Tô learned weaving and sewing, and she was a member of the school's musical group because she played the flute so well. However, the school only allowed her to play nice folk songs—songs about the beauty of rural life in peaceful times. She was not happy about this restriction and, instead, she played tunes which expressed her pain and hope, and the suffering and aspirations of thousands of children like her. She found it hard to understand why adults tried to hide the truth. Everywhere she and Stone Boy had gone, they had witnessed unfathomable suffering.

At Têt New Year, when everyone expected life in the cities to be peaceful and happy, there was the most terrifying destruction of all. Even in Saigon, entire neighborhoods of houses were destroyed, and putrefying corpses littered the streets. There were so many deaths that bulldozers had to be used to push the bodies into common graves. Hospitals overflowed with wounded adults and children. Even at Bien Hoa, Tô's school was shelled and several of her classmates were killed. This was the reality, yet everyone went on pretending that nothing of any grave consequence was happening.

Just the day before, as the school bus stopped in front of the City Hospital, she had heard a small girl singing a song by T.C. Son:

> I weep for the clouds asleep in the mountains.
> I weep for the trees on the rolling hills.
> I weep for my brothers, whose blood is running dry.
> I weep for our homeland, drenched with tears.
> I weep for the birds that have left the forest.
> I weep for the nights of funerals and wakes.
> I weep for my sisters, whose fate is sorrow.
> I weep for my teardrops, which have no name.

Tô could tell that the girl was about her own age and that she, too, was blind. Tô guessed that the person accompanying her on the zither was her father who had been handicapped by the war. "He probably has no other means of livelihood than to take his child to sing in the streets," Tô thought. As the little girl sang, Tô could hear the blind child's clarity about what was happening around her. It made Tô wonder what the adults had eyes for.

Just a day or two earlier Tô had had a strange dream about wandering with Stone Boy in search of Mother. It was a hot summer morning, and they were standing on a hill with seven or eight suns in the sky, and a moon and stars, too! She could not believe it—suns and stars at once! It was joyous, like a festival.

Suddenly, there were explosions, and the suns began to collapse and disintegrate as they landed. The sky went dark, and the moon and the stars disappeared. Cries of anguish could be heard from every direction, and she knew that these terrible things were happening because she had lost her mother. She knew that if she could find Mother, the suns would come back bright and hot in the sky, and the moon and stars would reappear too. She staggered in the dark, listening to cries of thousands of motherless children.

Then Stone Boy appeared out of nowhere with a sunflower in his hand—a big sunflower, as big as a Bien Hoa grapefruit filled with light—which he held up like a lamp to guide their way. Tô and Stone Boy went into villages and hamlets buried deep in darkness. At each place, Stone Boy raised his sunflower and sang. Once, they stopped in front of a row of houses crowded together, which appeared like a mountain, silent and cool in the dark night. Stone Boy raised his sunflower and sang. After a long while, a window opened, emitting a pale light. Dark figures gesturing to Stone Boy and Tô appeared at more and more windows. The children heard the growling of fierce wild animals. As the growling became louder and nearer, Tô took Stone Boy's hand, and they ran away.

The scene changed from a village to a dense forest. Stone Boy shone his luminous sunflower on every bush, tree, and stone. Then they were at the bottom of the ocean in the Kingdom of Waters, looking at every fish and blade of seaweed by the light of the flower. Tô and Stone Boy went everywhere, looking deeply at things. They met a very old man with snow white hair, who handed Stone Boy something big and round like a pumpkin. It shimmered like mother-of-pearl, and he called it the Sun of the Sea Palace. They could borrow it, he told them, and return to land to look for their mother. As Tô reached for the sparkling object, she woke up.

She tried to go back to sleep to continue the dream, but the sound of distant gunshots disturbed her. She sat up and opened her window. The cool air rushed in and refreshed her. She reached along the edge of her bed and found her flute. Raising it to her lips, she began to play very softly.

Tô played for a long time until she heard something besides her own music. It was the golden bird, with whom she had "conversed" for nine days in the forest. Tô was overjoyed as the bird told her that Stone Boy had arrived. She raised her flute and, by her music, asked the bird to confirm what she had understood. Yes, the bird was telling her that Stone Boy had returned. She put a jacket over her shoulders and, with flute in hand, opened the door and walked out into the yard. The golden bird hovered directly above her. Reaching the gate, she pulled back the latch, pushed it open and walked out. Then she heard someone calling out her name.

She turned. It was Stone Boy. He rushed to her and held her in his arms. Tô stood still and wept softly. Then they heard the bird crying in the sky, and Stone Boy told her, "Let's go now, before daylight." He took her hand, and the two children followed along the wall surrounding the school to find their way out of town. All the while, the golden bird hovered above them, pointing the way.

Tô wiped her eyes, and asked, "Where are we going now, Stone Boy?" Though only nine months had passed, Stone Boy seemed nine years older, and Tô was confident he would know the answer to her question.

"We'll get out of town first. Then we can try to find our way back to Dai Lao Forest. We must go back to our house and see whether Mother has come home. Then I must return to the mountain. I have been away for twelve moons now, you know."

"But how do you know which way to go? Home is so far away. We'll get lost."

"Don't worry, Tô. The golden bird will show us the way. He has been with me all the way from the mountains of Lang Son. He helped me find you, didn't he?"

Yes, Stone Boy had come to her all the way from the forests and mountains of the North. She was delirious with joy. If he had been able to find her, he would be able to find Mother, she thought.

Tô recalled the dream she had had the night before in which the white-bearded old man gave them a sun, as big as a pumpkin, shimmering like mother-of-pearl. She told Stone Boy about her dream, saying that perhaps the dream was a premonition of what was to come. She held Stone Boy's arm and walked close to him, and he listened to her every word. He asked her to tell him all that had happened since the day she was sent away to the School for the Blind at Bien Hoa. He listened in silence, except for occasional questions to clarify details. Soon they were outside the town, and heading deeper and deeper into a rubber tree forest. They walked all day with just two short rests. The golden bird fluttered overhead and faithfully accompanied them. Upon arriving at a man-made canal, they found an abandoned canoe and made it into a shelter for the night.

Tô and Stone Boy walked on for days towards the northwest. They crossed a forest of banana trees, full of ripe, succulent fruit, which they ate, along with fresh water from a nearby stream. Passing through a forest of bamboo trees, they broke some tender shoots and roasted them on a fire of dry bamboo leaves. They foraged in the jungle for days until they reached the clearing where months before they had seen soldiers camping on the stream bank, singing around a fire. Tô still remembered the man's sorrowful song about soldiers guarding lonely outposts far away from home.

During these days of walking, Stone Boy told Tô about his time at the School for Wards of the State. He had made friends with many other students whose fathers or brothers had died in battle. They formed a singing group to express their yearning for peace, and their songs touched everyone deeply, adults and children alike. Soon, however—perhaps the audiences' responses were too enthusiastic—the school's administration started dictating which songs could be sung. Stone Boy and his friends refused to sing these songs. Threats and punishments, then special favors and coaxing, could not sway them. Finally the school expelled Stone Boy, whom they considered the instigator, and sent him to a very strict Cadet School at Vung Tau.

At Cadet School, Stone Boy met many like-minded boys. One day, he and a group of his friends presented a petition to the school which stated that, instead of preparing to become fighters, they wanted to be trained as social workers. They could help villagers rebuild their homes, till the fields, and become part of the nationwide movement working for an early end to the war. The fact that students at a school for cadets should engage in such "subversive" activities was enough to create quite a stir, not only within the school itself but also in higher places. Stone Boy was charged with "propaganda for the enemy" and taken away to Chi Hoa Prison.

In prison, Stone Boy saw a number of Buddhist monks whose arms were in shackles. When he asked them what they had done, they told him they had publicly called on both sides to cease fire and discuss peaceful reconciliation, and for this they were imprisoned. During Stone Boy's second week at Chi Hoa, three hundred monks and nearly two hundred other prisoners began a hunger strike. One night Stone Boy was brutally awakened, brought to a room, and accused of inciting the monks to go on strike through his songs. Stone Boy was shackled and taken to a camp in Central Vietnam for political prisoners.

In the camp, Stone Boy met a very eccentric Taoist monk, whose hair was so long it covered both his ears. He was thin, even frail, but his eyes were sharp and brilliant. His brown peasant suit, after many washings, was the color of pale dirt. This unusual man always kept with him a cage containing a cat and two mice. It never ceased to amaze people that the cat never harmed the mice.

The old monk told Stone Boy that he had gone with his cage to the Provincial Headquarters and asked for an audience with the Commander. When he was denied entrance, he sat down at the main gate and refused to leave. People stopped and stared, and the old monk was only too happy to explain to anyone willing to listen, "I'm here to tell the government that if a cat can live in peace with two mice, why can't we human beings and compatriots live in peace together? We ought to stop killing one another this very day and start rebuilding our homeland."

Some people were moved to tears, but others railed at him, calling him stupid and naive. "No cat and mice can live together," they said. "This monk is crazy. Let them put him away." And indeed, the old monk ended up in prison.

Now he looked at Stone Boy, and pointed at his cage, "See, over a month they have been together and the cat has not eaten the mice, has it?"

Stone Boy enjoyed hearing the old monk tell stories. He said he had gone all over the villages in the East and collected bullets and bomb shrapnel to cast a big bell. Every night he would stay up late and invite the bell to sound in a slow, solemn manner. He had hoped that the sound of the bell would reach the heart of people and wake them up to the reality of the choice they were facing. He told Stone Boy, "By making those pieces of metal part of a temple bell, I helped them follow the peaceful way of a Buddha." Stone Boy was delighted by the image of deadly pieces of metal following the way of the Buddha, though he knew that such remarks could only confirm the suspicion that the old monk was indeed crazy.

The old monk and Stone Boy became close friends. At one point, they joined hundreds of other prisoners on a hunger strike. After a week, they were all taken to Quang Tri, the northernmost province of the South and ordered to walk north onto a bridge over Ben Hai, the river that separated North and South Vietnam. A southern officer, in a camouflage suit, said to them as they were leaving, "Go on! Over there you'll have plenty of chances for hunger strikes."

As they reached the other end of the bridge, they were warmly greeted by the authorities and people of the North. When they were asked why they were expelled from the South, the old monk

and Stone Boy told the simple truth, which everyone seemed pleased to hear. Later, in private, an
official told Stone Boy that he should say that people in the South were leading a miserable existence, and that people in the North should send
their young men south to save their fellow coun-
trymen, and that the foreign soldiers must be
forced out of the country.

Stone Boy listened carefully but he knew they
were not speaking the truth. Yes, in the South there
were people who exploited others and enriched
themselves while thousands of soldiers and civilians were dying every day. It was true that the authorities in the South did everything in their
power to hide the truth about the war and to crush
anyone who had the courage to call for negotia-
tions for an end to this fratricide. But the people in
the South also suffered immeasurably because of
the soldiers who came down from the North. Millions of people lost their homes, their loved ones,
and even their own lives because of this clash between brothers. The real pain was shared by people
of the same race and same history who were unable
to sit down and resolve their differences. This was
the real cause of the suffering, not this or that ex-
ploitative foreign power, even though the guns and
bullets both sides were using to destroy each other
were brought by outsiders. After the authorities de-
parted, Stone Boy revealed his thoughts about the
war to the old Taoist monk. The old monk nodded
in accord.

During the following days, the monk and Stone
Boy went into hamlets and villages and visited
with the ordinary country people of the North. Ev-

erywhere they went, they saw people living in poverty, though there was not as much destruction as they had seen in the South. There seemed to be only the very old and the very young in the hamlets. The able-bodied were all in the armed forces.

When the people heard Stone Boy talk about the real situation in the South, they realized they had been deceived. They had trusted that their sons and brothers had gone South to fight foreign invaders. They had no idea that brothers were killing brothers. After discussing the situation among themselves, the villagers decided to go to the Provincial Committee and demand that their sons be allowed to come home. Old ladies wept openly and hugged Stone Boy, telling him that their sons had been killed in battle, they knew not where. The local cadres reported this to their higher-ups, and the old monk and Stone Boy were separated and taken away. The Taoist monk held Stone Boy's hand in his and laughed heartily. He recited a short poem—witty, ironic, and delightful—about being constant and courageous, and keeping a sense of humor in face of adversity.

Stone Boy was taken to a re-education camp where he had to do strenuous physical labor with little food or sleep. Absolute obedience was the rule. During study periods, he was only permitted to listen and remember what he was told, and he was not allowed to speak up or present anything of his own that ran counter to the official line. Stone Boy was shocked to find out that in the North there was as much cover-up of the truth as in the South. Perhaps the official lies were even more complete and the discipline more harsh in the North. He realized, too, that even if he were permitted to speak up, it would have been to no avail. People at the "citizens' meetings" (convened by the authorities themselves) raised their arms or brought them down like automatons. They had been trained to do so for a long time. He saw, too, that while they moved their arms up or down—to applaud or condemn this or that—their faces were impassive, betraying no emotion whatsoever, only resignation and acceptance.

One day during a "political study session," in which the air was stifling like the sky before a summer storm, Stone Boy began to sing. Everyone turned towards him and stopped listening to the formal speaker. At first the speaker was infuriated, but after a while, the song entered him, and he sat down with bent head and listened along with everyone else.

Stone Boy was transferred to another re-education camp. His punishment was to walk from Ha Tinh to a camp in the harsh mountain region of Lang Son Province, where inmates were deprived of even the most basic health care and nutrition, and many became partially paralyzed, blind, or gangrenous because of neglect.

One day, while Stone Boy was cutting wood in the forest under the watchful eye of a cadre, he felt an urge to return to his mountain home. Suddenly, a high mountain appeared against the deep, blue sky. Huge boulders formed a stony point that jutted out from the mountain. Every night, dew would collect in a crevice the size of a sunflower. One sip of this miraculous water, and the pain, thirst, and torments of a thousand lives would dissolve.

Stone Boy thought that if Tô could climb up that mountain, take a sip of that water, and wash her eyes with it, she would be able to see again. As Stone Boy thought this, he began to sing. The cadre looked at him in disbelief and suddenly, from all corners of the forest, came the sound of wings beating. Birds filled the sky. Then Stone Boy heard the cries of the golden bird. He raised his voice and asked the bird to lead him to his friend Tô.

Stone Boy and the golden bird took two weeks to reach Bien Hoa. As they approached the School for the Blind, Stone Boy heard the familiar sound of Tô's flute. When Tô walked out the gate, Stone Boy told her about the crevice in the rock filled with the miraculous dew which could heal her eyes. As Tô felt a great hope rise within her, she realized that the water had already begun to have its healing effect.

Tô and Stone Boy chatted so excitedly that they reached the Upper Village without even knowing it. Their old village looked very dilapidated and vacant. Stone Boy could see that the war had not spared even this humble corner. He identified Tô's old house and cried with joy. Tô raised her hand to her chest and felt her heart beat wildly. She asked him, "Is it still standing, Stone Boy? Do you think Ma is in there?"

Stone Boy could see that the house was intact, but there was no one in sight. They crossed the stream and followed the path up the hillside. Stone Boy pushed back the bamboo door, and led her inside. Now Tô no longer needed a guide, for she knew every inch of that little house. She went straight to the kitchen, then to the water basin in the back, and finally to the vegetable patch. But everywhere she went, she felt only voidness. It was obvious that her mother had never come back from the marketplace since that Wednesday many months ago. Overcome with grief, Tô went out and sat on the doorstep.

Stone Boy asked her to walk with him to the stream. He reminded Tô that they had freed two fishes there—one orange and the other silver. "You know, they also started their journey the same day we did. I wonder whether they have found their mother. If so, we might see them here again."

Tô could see, in her mind's eye, the two tiny fishes swimming together. She hoped that they had not been separated from each other during their search for their mother. If they had been, she hoped that they would be reunited as she and Stone Boy were now. A smile formed on her lips as she remembered how the two fishes had been as small as two fingers. A year had now passed; they must be as big as her hand!

Stone Boy and Tô spent the night in the little house. The next morning, they got up early and walked towards the Dai Lao Forest, from which they could walk to the summit of the mountain. The path became steeper and steeper until Stone Boy could no longer see the golden bird, but he did not need a guide anymore. It became increasingly difficult to climb, especially for Tô, but they continued. After three arduous days, as dusk fell, they reached the base of the summit.

"Only a little way further, Tô. But let's rest here," he said, leading her to a large, flat rock and inviting her to sit down. When Stone Boy saw that Tô's brow was drenched with sweat, he picked up a large leaf and fanned her with it. Tô sat and breathed deeply for a while and began to feel rested and happy. She realized that the air around her was extraordinarily clean and cool. Tô noticed a fragrance and wondered whether it was of plants and flowers, or of the sky and clouds themselves. She felt a lightness, a floating sensation. This was the land of Stone Boy's birth.

She asked him, "Are there any houses up here, Stone Boy? You will take me to your house, won't you? To meet your father and mother? They'll be so glad to see you again."

Stone Boy remembered how he had found it difficult to say anything the first time Tô and her mother asked him about his home and family. They thought it was too painful for him to talk about the parents he had lost, and they did not persist. But now, Stone Boy thought, he must tell the truth. He put down the big leaf and told Tô, "This is where I come from. That's all I know. I don't have a father and a mother the way you did. There are no houses up here. I was born a long time ago. It is possible that since I was born, the full moon has gone over the summit of this mountain one thousand times, or perhaps ten thousand times. I sit here days and nights listening only to the songs of the sky, the clouds, the rain, the wind, the flowers, and the birds. Though no one has taught me, I know how to sing."

"But every child has a father and a mother. You must have parents. Who are they?"

"As I said, I do not know. Perhaps Heaven and Earth gave me birth. Or perhaps the stones brought me here. But look, Tô, I do have a mother! My mother is Mrs. Ba Ty, your mother, your loving, wonderful Ma. You and I, we are Ma's children. We just spent a year looking for her!"

A tear pearled on Tô's eyelashes. She realized that Stone Boy was right. When Mother gave birth to her, she also gave birth to Heaven and Earth, houses and trees. Were there no Mother, how could there be forests, fields, grasses, and flowers? Without Mother, how could there be Stone Boy himself? Now it seemed obvious to Tô that Stone Boy had indeed come into the world thanks to her mother. Even the two little fishes had been given birth by Mother, so they too were now looking for her. Without lifting her head, Tô said, "Stone Boy, do you think we'll ever find Ma?"

"Yes, of course I do. We'll find her. She cannot be dead and gone and lost forever. She has given birth to Heaven and Earth, forests and fields. If they are still here, so is she. There is only one thing that we must do, and that is to find her. Once we have found her, everything will be all right. Once we have found her, people will no longer kill one another, villages will no longer be destroyed, and children will no longer be lost. I am looking for Mother. You are looking for Mother. The two little fishes are looking for her, too. Even the old Taoist monk is looking for her. And I think she, too, is looking for us. Yes, Tô, don't you think so? Ma cannot be dead and gone forever. One day we will find her." Tô did not speak. Ever since she had come to know Stone Boy, she had always believed what he said. And he was speaking to her again.

"I used to sit up here and listen to the sounds of your flute wafting up from the forest below. I could hear you as well as if you were sitting next to me. I heard your music, and I knew you were in pain. That was why I came down from the mountain. I came down and sang for you, and served as your eyes, your guide. We were two persons, yet we walked together and became one person. In truth, you and I are one, because I am within you and you are within me. You may not see this now, but one day you will. And once you have understood this, wherever you go in this world, you will see that I am with you.

"Look, the moon is almost perfectly round tonight. This is the full moon day of the fourth month. Last year on this day, I came down the mountain. Are you rested now? It is just a short walk from here to the top." Tô stood up. Stone Boy offered his arm, and the two children walked under the bright moonlight.

A short time later, they reached the summit. Stone Boy found a place for Tô to sit with her back against a flat rock. It was perfectly still. Tô felt as if the entire forest were very far away, and that the flat rock was a small island surrounded by the vast ocean. The wind blew softly and brushed against Tô's face, making her cheeks cool, almost cold. The dew was falling. Tô heard Stone Boy's approaching footsteps, then his voice.

"We've got to wait until midnight for the dew to collect enough. . . " Stone Boy interrupted himself and went back to sit next to Tô, saying, "The moon is very bright here, but down below the mist obscures everything. There is mist up here, too, but it's very light and we can still see the stars. Time has flown, hasn't it? Twelve full moons like this since I left my mountain!"

Putting his hand on Tô's shoulder, he continued, "Tomorrow, we can follow the direction of the rising sun to return home. You will want to stop at the stream and see if the little fishes have come back, won't you? What are you thinking, Tô?"

Tô replied, "I am thinking about the dream I had the night you came to the School for the Blind. You were holding a big sunflower which emitted a pale light, just bright enough for us to see our way ahead. Yes, I was able to see as if I were not blind at all. Oh, brother Stone Boy, I am no longer a blind girl with you next to me. You are my eyes."

The moon was directly above the children. It was midnight, and very still. Stone Boy went to look at the stone hollow.

"Tô, it is full of dew now."

Stone Boy returned to help Tô make her way slowly up the treacherous path to the summit. When they reached it, Stone Boy explained, "This is miraculous dew, my sister. I will scoop it up for you to drink and wash your eyes. You will feel better than you ever have before. You'll be able to go for months without food or water, and your body will be healthy and your mind clear. This dew will give you back your eyesight."

Stone Boy carefully cupped his hands and filled them with the miraculous dew. It seemed to Tô as if time had paused, as if above her the moon and the stars were watching her in great solemnity. The old man with the white beard, whom Tô had met in the Kingdom of Waters, was standing next to Stone Boy, about to hand her a big sunflower. Tô knelt down on the stone, and her knees began to shake lightly. Stone Boy brought his hands to her lips, and she drank the dew with utmost respect. Tô felt transformed, and a sense of ease welled up in her and spread throughout her body. She breathed long, deep breaths, and she felt all her fears, worries, and pain dissolve. Again and again, Stone Boy cupped his hands and scooped up the precious dew to wash Tô's eyes.

Then he led her to a big flat rock, and as she lay down, he placed his jacket over her and said, "Cover your forehead, or the cold dew will give you a headache. You can go to sleep now. I am right here."

Tô lay very still and listened to the stillness that surrounded her. She again felt as if she were on a small island adrift in the ocean. The wind rustled far away. She heard an occasional drop of dew falling to the ground, and she was aware of Stone Boy's regular and light breathing. She said to herself she ought to go to sleep too, but she went on listening to Stone Boy's breathing which seemed to merge with the breathing of the gentle wind.

❋   ❋   ❋

Tô awoke to the sound of birds singing. She brought one hand to her eyes, and was struck by a strange yet familiar impression. It was the sunlight! She was no longer blind. Stone Boy had indeed helped her regain her eyesight. Tô put her hands over her eyes, the light was so glaring, but she tried to see between her fingers. Here and there, she could see the stones, the sky. A moment later, she dropped her hands from her face.

The first thing she saw was an immense rock, three or four times as large as her parents' house. It was standing upright against a vast, clear blue, cloudless sky, which spread over and beyond the summit, and curved down on all sides of the mountain. She stood on a lone island.

Tô turned around and saw that the forest and the mountains below were still bathed in the morning mist. The immensity and depth made her feel she had escaped an existence full of suffering and sorrow.

She looked around but did not see Stone Boy. She called his name, and the sound of her voice rolled into space, touching the trees, the mist, the stones, and echoed back to her. There was still no response. She called his name again with all her strength, but no one replied.

Tô began to panic. She climbed up the nearest rock and looked in the direction of the rising sun. There was no sign of anyone. Then her eyes caught a vision at the very top of the highest peak which took her breath away. The rock had the shape, the form, the bearing that was Stone Boy's. Yes, it *was* Stone Boy, and he was waving to her.

How strange, for when she was blind she had never seen Stone Boy, yet she recognized him in the shape of the rock. It was an image she had previously formed while listening to the sound of his voice and feeling the lines and shapes of his face. Now for the first time, perhaps the only time, she could see him with her own eyes.

Tô rubbed her eyelids and looked again. The stony figure was no longer waving to her. Though it still resembled Stone Boy, he had gone back to where he had come from. He had again become stone.

"Days and nights, I sit on the summit of the mountain, and listen to the songs of the sky, the clouds, the rain, the wind, the flowers, and the birds. Though no one has taught me, I know how to sing." Now Tô understood what Stone Boy had said the day before. "I was born a long time ago...Since I was born, the full moon has gone over the summit of this mountain one thousand times, perhaps ten thousand times."

"Stone Boy has left me all alone in the world," she thought. "He came to be with me, why didn't he stay with me forever?"

"In truth, you and I are one, because I am within you, and you are within me. You do not see this now but one day soon you will understand. And once you understand this, wherever you go in this world, you will see that I am with you."

Tô bent down and wept, for she was, after all, only a child. She cried until the sun rose and hung above her head. She had no doubt now that Stone Boy had left her forever. He never really loved her, she thought. Her own mother had left her. And now even Stone Boy had left her. Alone, how could she ever find her Ma?

She suddenly wished she were blind again so that Stone Boy would be with her, talk to her, and let her touch his hand and face. With tears in her eyes, she brought her flute to her lips and poured all her pain into her music. Even the clouds flying past the mountain stopped and gathered around. The golden bird returned and began to sing. Tô stopped playing and listened. Though it was a bird's song, she knew what it was singing to her:

> Do you remember the day
>> our Mother first brought me here?
> Through the five rivers, I have come to you.
> But one day, when you no longer see me,
>> smile, and quietly look for me
>> in all the things that come and go.
> You will find that I am
>> that which never comes
>> and never goes.
> I am that reality beyond time,
>> beyond perception.

Tô listened to the golden bird's song, and she knew these were Stone Boy's own words. Though she did not understand the meaning, she tried to inscribe them in her mind and heart, so that she would never forget them. She raised her flute and played, asking the bird why Stone Boy had gone away. But the bird only sang the same song again.

Tô knew the bird had one message to tell her. There was no way she could learn anything more. Slowly, she put down her flute. Without Stone Boy, how could she go down the mountain alone? Then a light flashed through her mind. "Now," she said to herself, "I have regained my eyesight, so I can go down the mountain by myself!" Only the day before, she recalled, she had said to Stone Boy, "Brother, when you are with me, I am no longer blind. You are my eyes." Stone Boy would always be present for Tô now that she could see.

She understood what Stone Boy had said to her, "In truth, you and I are one, because I am within you, and you are within me. You may not see this now, but one day soon, you will. Once you understand this, you will see that I am present with you wherever you go."

A warm teardrop rolled down her cheek, soothing her heart full of sorrow. No wonder Stone Boy had told her, "Tomorrow, we will follow the direction of the rising sun and return home." "Of course Stone Boy is with me," she thought.

Tô raised her head and looked at the sky, the clouds, the rocks, and the trees. She knew that Stone Boy was also looking at them, seeing them, and transmitting their images to her eyes. The sounds of trees and the wind were his voice. She had only to listen, and she could hear him. From then on, she knew that not only was Stone Boy within her, but he was present everywhere.

The rocky peak on the mountain top was indeed Stone Boy. No, Tô was not going down the mountain now. She wanted to stay here for the rest of the day. There was time, for now she had faith in what Stone Boy had told her. Her Ma was alive, and she would find her. She would go—not alone, for Stone Boy would be with her—and they would find Mother, just as the two little fishes had done, just as the old monk had done. Tô was sure that the day of finding Mother would be a day all wars would stop—people would stop killing one another, destroying each other's houses, and causing so many children to wander around like stray animals.

Tô wanted to show Stone Boy that she truly understood what he had taught her, so she raised her flute to her lips and played. Sky and clouds, mountain and trees, settled down in peace and listened to her song.

A Lone Pink Fish

A Lone Pink Fish

A lone pink fish swims quickly in the South China Sea. The waves reflect the glint of her bright, sunlit scales as she rises to the surface. Fishing boats seldom encounter this fish. Her secret is well kept. In fact, only one person knows her mission, and that is a young Vietnamese woman named Dao.

Dao is nineteen and, together with the young man she loved and forty-two others, she left Vietnam on a small boat. On their way past Quai Island, off the Thai coast, they were attacked by pirates who stole everything they had and raped all the women aboard. Dao was violated by three of them, one after another. The men aboard tried desperately to protect the women, but they were no match for the pirates who beat and bound them. Dao's fiancé also endured this fate.

Terrified, Dao kicked and screamed. When she scratched her third attacker, he grabbed her by the leg and hurled her into the sea. Her cries, along with her body, were swallowed up by the ocean and she lost consciousness. But Dao did not drown. She was rescued by the pink fish who carried her to a sandy beach on a tiny, deserted island.

When Dao regained consciousness, she noticed that her body was badly bruised, and it took all of her strength just to sit up. Waves lapped onto the shore close to her feet. She struggled to stand and then staggered towards some boulders that offered shade. Heaving a sigh, she collapsed against one of the boulders and marveled that she was still alive.

Slowly, she recalled all that had happened. She cradled her head in her arms and dared not look out at the sea for fear the pirates were still there. But no, the terrifying scene of the previous day had passed. When she finally lifted her head, she saw only the vast, endless sea. As she thought of the pirates' cruelties, tears streamed down her cheeks. She looked at her aching body. Not a shred of clothing remained. Ashamed, she covered her breasts with her arms and looked up again. Sunlight shimmered on the sea. The deep blue sky was cloudless. There was no sign of any vessel. No black dot was visible in any direction.

Dao thought of Dat, the young man she loved, and she agonized that he must have been beaten and killed by the pirates. Wrapping her arms around herself, gasping for air, Dao sobbed. Her arms went limp, and she fell to the ground. Feeling her strength seep away, Dao was sure that she would cease breathing and die alone on the deserted island. But to her surprise, her breathing regained an even rhythm, and she fell into a deep sleep. She did not wake up until the radiant moon shone in the vast sky.

Dao felt a small hand touch her forehead. A young girl, ten or eleven years old, wearing a pink shirt and frayed white pants, was standing above her. She had bright black eyes and hair that brushed her shoulders.

"Who are you? Why are you here at this hour?" Dao asked anxiously.

Calmly the child answered, "My name is Hong. I arrived as the sun was setting."

The young girl reached over and pulled some clothes off a branch, and handed them to Dao. "Put these on so you won't get cold, elder sister. Then we can talk. It's already getting misty, and look, you're shivering."

Dazed and bewildered, Dao took a pair of Vietnamese pants and a blouse still fragrant with camphor. As Dao buttoned her blouse, she wondered, "Who is this child alone at night on this island? Is she a ghost come to haunt me?"

As this doubt crossed Dao's mind, the child spoke, "I'm not a ghost, elder sister. I'm a real person. I was born in Vinh Long, where my parents were merchants for almost twenty years. Come, sit down and eat some of these crackers while we talk."

As Dao sat beside her, Hong opened a large tin canister and took out a plastic bag filled with crackers. She tore the bag open with her teeth, and handed two crackers to Dao. Dao's stomach rumbled. She hadn't eaten a thing in nearly two days. The crackers were the kind on which she and her friends had always spread sweetened condensed milk. Each cracker was four fingers wide. After eating one, Dao asked, "Where did you get these?"

Hong laughed, "This is one of several tins a Danish ship threw into the sea. Go ahead and eat another while I tell you about it. You see, today there was a refugee boat that ran out of food and drinking water. The boat's motor had died. Most of the eighty-four people aboard were children. A ship bearing the French flag approached. The refugees waved their shirts and cried for help, but the French captain pretended not to see them. Several hours later, a British ship passed by, but they too pretended not to see the refugees. Just before sundown, a ship flying the Danish flag came near. Hearing the cries for help, the ship circled the refugee boat three times. They did not want to take the refugees aboard, but they did drop down two barrels of water and ten canisters of crackers. Seven tins fell onto the boat, and three fell into the sea. This canister is one of those."

Dao asked, "Did the boat meet any ship after that? And did they finally make it to shore? Were you one of those aboard? Where are the others? Did the boat sink and everyone else drown?"

"You ask so many questions I feel dizzy! No, I was not aboard that boat. And it has not sunk yet. In fact, right now the northeasterly wind is blowing it towards Thailand. I think they will make it safely to shore."

Hong's face grew sad. Dao wanted to ask Hong more, but she hesitated. "How does this young child know so much?" Dao puzzled. "And how extraordinary is her calm, mature bearing and manner of speaking. A normal ten-year-old, lost on a deserted island, far from her family, would never speak so serenely and matter-of-factly. It would seem more natural for such a young child to cling to me as an older sister and cry out for her mother. Yet here she is taking care of me as though she were the elder sister, giving me clothes to wear and food to eat. Perhaps I'm dreaming," thought Dao, and she bit her lip until it drew blood.

Just then, Hong raised one finger and gestured to Dao, "Listen, I think I hear running water. Maybe we can find fresh water to drink. Please stay here while I look."

Hong skipped lightly over the rocks, and vanished among the dark shadows of the jungle trees. Waiting for Hong to return, Dao reached into the bag for two more crackers and ate them slowly. Hong returned holding a large leaf folded into a cup brimming with clear water.

"This water is fresh. Here, drink some."

Hong lifted the leaf cup to Dao's lips. The sweet water refreshed Dao all the way down to her stomach.

"Go ahead, drink it all. I've already had some."

Dao emptied the leaf cup and thanked Hong.

Hong told her, "Near the spring there is an enclosure sheltered from the wind where we can sleep. It's too cold to stay here, and the tide might come in during the night and take us out to sea."

Hong put the crackers back into the tin and handed it to Dao. She lifted the bag of clothes and proceeded down a rocky path leading to the spring. The moonlight shone brilliantly over the whole island.

At one place near the spring, Hong waited for Dao to sit down and then she spoke, "We were lucky to find water. With our tin of Danish crackers, we'll be fine for at least a couple of weeks. We can also look for fruit and edible plants. We must keep a lookout for any refugee boat that might pass by, so we can signal them to rescue us. I scavenged a bundle of clothes while you were sleeping. I thought the shirt and pants would fit you, so I hung them up on that tree branch to dry. We can dry out the other clothes to use as blankets. Now, if you're not too tired, elder sister, tell me your story."

Dao told Hong how she had become a boat refugee. In 1976, her father, a writer, was sent to a re-education camp in the northern highlands of Vietnam. Two years passed before Dao's mother could save enough money to visit him. She found him thin and wasted and deeply depressed. He urged his wife to take their children and escape to another country, but Dao's mother refused to abandon her husband and told her friends, "There is a saying, 'As long as there is water, a harvest is possible.' Just so, as long as my husband is alive, I will wait for him."

Afterwards, she and her mother could only afford to send him a letter, a small packet of sugar, and a bottle of salt once every three months. Sometimes six or seven months would pass with no news from him.

Life grew harsher with each passing day. Dao and her sixteen-year-old brother tried their best to help their mother earn a living as a vendor. But they could not make enough money to feed the family.

Dao had a friend named Nguyen, whose family was also poor, but they managed well, thanks to relatives overseas who sent them packages every two months. The parcels contained cigarettes, canned butter, and antibiotics, which they could sell to buy rice and other necessities.

When Dao's fiancé suggested that they try to escape by boat, Dao could not make up her mind. She did not fear for her own life, but she was afraid her mother could not survive without her. One night, her mother held her close and, weeping, urged Dao to go. Dao left everything she owned with her mother. All she took was her high school diploma and the clothes she had on. She stayed up late with her brother the night before she left, and asked him to take care of the family. "As soon as I reach Malaysia," she said, "I'll send you a telegram."

But the engine of their boat broke down in the middle of the sea, and they were tossed about for sixteen days and nights, leaving them prey to an attack by sea pirates. Images of the rapes, beatings, and violence loomed up in Dao's mind, and she covered her face. Tears fell like rain as she recalled Dat's suffering and her own, as well as the suffering of everyone aboard. She cried for her mother, her brother, and the man she loved. In desperation, she screamed, "I will beat my head against these rocks until I kill myself!"

Hong was listening quietly, now and then squeezing Dao's hand in her own, but she did not interrupt her. When Dao jumped up to bash her head against the rocks, Hong held her with such unusual strength that Dao could not move, and she fell to her knees. Though the night air was chilly, Dao was covered with sweat. Hong gently helped her onto the grass and used her sleeve to wipe the perspiration from Dao's forehead.

She waited until Dao's pain eased before saying softly, "Dao, please think of your parents, your brothers, and your sisters before you destroy yourself. They would suffer all their lives thinking you had drowned at sea. You have a good chance of being rescued by another refugee boat and making it to land, where you will be able to find work and help your family. Just knowing that you reached shore safely will give your parents happiness the rest of their lives. And the others aboard your boat also have a good chance of reaching shore safely. The pirates left after they threw you overboard. I saw your boat being carried by the waves towards the southwest. In just a few days, it will probably reach Malaysia. Dat is still alive, and you may meet him again."

Dao clutched Hong's arm. "Are you sure? Are you sure Dat is still alive? How could you have seen his boat? Where were you? What boat were you on? Where are your parents?"

Hong said, "I promise to tell you everything tomorrow. My story is like yours. But it's very late, and we should sleep so we can get up early and look for boats. Please lie down. You can use the root of this tree as a pillow."

Dao joined her palms and said, "I pray with all my heart that Dat is still alive." She paused and, with an agonized expression, continued, "But, little sister, my body is spoiled now. I am no longer worthy of Dat. It's horribly unjust how a woman preserves herself carefully for her future husband, and then in seconds everything is ruined by a pirate. There is nothing left for me to live for."

Dao wept bitterly. Slowly, Hong spoke, "Many people live, not for pleasure, but for responsibility and love. Living for responsibility and love can be a source of great happiness, elder sister."

In her misery, Dao could not grasp the deep meaning of Hong's words. But because they were unusual words to come from one so young, Dao listened attentively, somewhat awestruck, as Hong continued, "Who knows how many people have drowned and had their flesh ripped and devoured by sharks? But the ocean is not the only place where sharks are found, elder sister. There are sharks on land who devour flesh and bones in order to survive. Pirates are a kind of shark. Perhaps because they suffer on land from other sharks, they in turn become sharks on the sea. Sharks swimming in the sea have devoured tens of thousands of our people. Sharks on boats have attacked tens of thousands more. You were attacked by three such sharks.

"You endured one part of our people's great suffering. Who among us has not been wounded? Who among us has been able to keep our body and spirit intact? In my eyes, you are still pure and chaste, Dao. The pirates attacked you and forced themselves upon you, but they could not really take anything from you. You never consented to give your body to them. You bear no blame. Your wounds will heal one day, like the wounds of someone who has survived a shark attack. It is essential that you not allow your wounds to become infected with poison. Wounds can poison your spirit as well as your body. In ten days or so, you will make it to shore, and there you can find a doctor who can prevent the poison from infecting your body. But no doctor can heal the wounds of your spirit. That is up to you."

Each of Hong's words touched Dao's heart. Her tears flowed, and she felt lighter inside. After a few moments, Hong said, "When I was still in Vietnam, my grandmother used to chant the *Heart of Perfect*

Understanding Sutra. I didn't understand the words, but whenever I heard them, I felt refreshed inside. You are so tired and sad. Let me chant the sutra for you."

Hong began to chant without waiting for Dao to respond. As Dao listened, she felt the pain within her subside. Tears as sweet as dew rolled down her cheeks. Hong had not yet finished chanting the sutra a fourth time when Dao fell into a deep sleep. She did not stir again until the sun rose.

When Dao opened her eyes, Hong was not there. Guessing that Hong had gone off exploring, Dao washed her face in the spring water and rinsed the salt from her hair. Then she climbed onto a large boulder and looked out in all directions. Sunlight poured across the sea and lit up the small island. There was not a cloud in sight. A sudden pain in her stomach reminded Dao of her hunger, and she walked back to get a cracker from the tin. She took small bites and chewed slowly and carefully. The cracker was fragrant and buttery, truly delicious. She only ate one, for fear they would not last, and she scooped up a handful of water and drank until her stomach was full.

Then she opened the bundle of clothes and saw a purple blouse, a sweater the color of milk, a large yellow towel, and a child's shirt the shade of incense smoke. "This will fit Hong," she thought as she carried the shirt and other things back to the spring to wash them. After rinsing the salt from the clothes, she wrung them out and laid them on the rocks to dry. Hong still had not returned. Dao called Hong's name, but there was no response. "Where could she be?" Dao worried. She followed the stream up to the top of the island, stepping carefully on patches of grass and smooth stones to protect her tender bare feet.

The island was densely covered with wild, tropical plants. Dao picked a leaf from a guava tree and crushed it in her fingers to smell its pungent fragrance. She felt as if she had just met an old friend. She remembered her grandmother's guava tree in Can Tho. As a child, Dao had often climbed it and sat among the branches eating the fruit and smelling the leaves. Her grandmother used to scold her, "Girls do not climb trees!" Dao never could understand this admonition, and so she continued to climb trees, but in secret.

Climbing along the guava branches was always great fun, as the flexible branches never broke. Her brother once fell when a plumeria branch cracked. Dao knew that the plumeria branches were brittle so she never climbed on them, even though the flowers were so fragrant. Besides, the plumeria tree was right in front of the house, and she did not want to be caught climbing trees.

Dao was happy to see a familiar guava tree in a place so strange to her. Although there were only a few fruits, and they were out of reach and not yet ripe, she longed for a taste. First she looked around to make sure no one was watching. "How funny," she thought, "to worry about being caught climbing a tree on a deserted island!" She grabbed a branch to climb up, but her strength failed her. So she broke off a low, dry branch, pulled down one of the higher branches with it, and plucked one unripe fruit. It was quite sour, but the familiar taste filled her heart with joy. She had been separated from her homeland only two weeks and from the people on her boat merely a day, but she felt cut off from everything she had ever known.

Thanks to this guava tree, she realized that she was still standing on the familiar green earth. Dao looked ahead, out over the sea. The sun was to her left, so she must have come from the east. She must not be too far from the coast of Thailand. Dat's boat was drifting towards Malaysia. She believed everything Hong had told her, as if Hong possessed a special knowledge. How strange this child was who acted and spoke like an adult! The more Dao thought about it, the stranger it seemed. Many changes had taken place in Dao's heart since yesterday, and they were all thanks to this little girl. If Hong had not been present, Dao probably would have thrown herself against the rocks and ended her life. How could a ten-year-old, eleven at most, speak with such authority? "You've endured one part of the terrible sufferings that our people have had to endure. Who among us has not been wounded? Who among us has been able to keep wholly intact our body and spirit? To me you are still pure and chaste. The pirates attacked you, but they could not really take anything away from you. Your wounds are like the wounds from a shark attack."

These words, containing such deep understanding, soothed the pain in Dao's heart. A ten-year-old girl had taught her more in one day than she had learned in all her years of school. But who was Hong? And why did she refuse to answer Dao's questions about how she had made it alone to the island with a tin of crackers and a bundle of

clothes? How did she know Dat's boat was being
blown towards the southwest? And how could a
ten-year-old be so much more serene and wise than
a nineteen-year-old like herself? Was Hong a supernatural being? Dao shivered at the thought,
even as the warm sunlight streamed down across
her face.

She went back to see if the clothes and tin of
crackers were indeed real. Were they only sticks
and stones a ghost had transformed to trick her?
No, Hong could not be a ghost. Dao had as proof the
very clothes she was wearing, which Hong had
given her the day before. Dao remembered clearly
that she had awakened without a stitch of clothing
on, and she could see the clothes she had just
rinsed drying in the sun. Dao gathered the dry
clothes and folded them neatly. "No, Hong could
not be a ghost," Dao thought. "But where was she
now? Why hadn't she returned?" Dao climbed up
on a high rock for a better view, when she heard
Hong's laughter from along the shore. Then she
saw Hong coming up from the water, yet Dao noticed that Hong's clothes were perfectly dry.

Without dwelling on this strange fact, Dao was
elated, and all her worries vanished the moment
she heard Hong's childish laughter, bright and
clear. Dao called, "Where were you? It's past noon.
I've been looking everywhere for you!"

Hong stood beside Dao and pointed to the black
clouds gathering. "There's going to be a storm, elder sister. We'd better find shelter."

Hong led Dao towards the huge boulders, and
they found a large, dry cave. "Sit here, elder sister.
I'll go back and get our crackers and clothes."

Dao brushed away the pebbles on the cave floor, and cleared a place to sit. She leaned back against the rock wall. Outside, the sky grew very dark. Large raindrops fell as though someone were hurling down heavy stones from above. Lightning flashed across the sky, followed by an explosive clap of thunder so loud it seemed immediately overhead. When Hong returned, Dao hugged her close and brushed the rain from her hair and shirt. The young girl let Dao take care of her. The rain outside rushed down like a waterfall, but the two girls stayed safe and dry inside their cave. They both were thinking about how rough and choppy the ocean must be in the storm. Slowly Hong opened her eyes and said, "When the sea is like this, many refugee boats sink."

Dao listened solemnly. In her mind, she could see boats filled with frightened men, women, and children, tossed about by monstrous waves; arms waving frantically, terrified cries lost in the howling wind; bodies sinking beneath the water where sharks circled. Trembling, she felt as if her heart were being squeezed by a cruel hand, and she asked herself why her people had had to endure such suffering day after day for more than fifty years. She looked at Hong and saw the child's cheeks stained with tears. Seeing Hong weep made her own pain subside, and she felt the cruel hand release its grip on her heart. She wiped Hong's tears away with her shirt sleeve, and the two girls sat quietly together, as dark clouds raced across the sky and the wind howled. Lying in Dao's arms, Hong closed her eyes and slept. Her breathing grew light and even. Dao felt as though she was holding everything she had ever loved.

The rain continued until late in the afternoon. Finally, the clouds passed, the sky grew quiet, and the sun began to shine. The island looked refreshed. Dao and Hong helped each other up onto a large boulder and looked out across the horizon. There was no sign of any boat. Dao pulled Hong down onto the rock and asked her to tell her story.

Hong looked troubled for a moment, and then replied, "I'll tell you my whole story, but only if you let me tell it in two parts—part now and the rest tomorrow. Do you agree?"

Dao nodded in assent. After a moment of silence, Hong began, "When I was a baby, my world was only as big as my mother's two arms. Safe in that world, I felt secure and peaceful. I did not know that beyond those protective arms lay a universe of violence and storms. My mother kept that world from my view so that I might enjoy endless peace and safety. But recently I have seen the world outside.

"Back in Vinh Long, my parents had an ice store and a small grocery. They were good, generous people, well loved by their customers and employees. My parents also tended a fruit orchard of more than five hundred mango, longan, and durian trees. But my father was killed by a soldier's stray bullet, and our grocery store was destroyed by bombs. Mother was two months pregnant when Father was killed, and soon afterwards she gave birth to a beautiful boy. My little brother, named Bich, looked exactly like my father. Mother and I cherished Bich. When the Provisional Government

of South Vietnam came to power, my mother decided to return to the countryside. I started attend-
ing the village school, and every afternoon Mother
would carry Bich to meet me at school. Then we
would stroll among the mango and longan trees.

"Mother gave the ice store and all her money to
the local officials for the state. She wanted only to
retain the fruit orchard, as we could easily support
ourselves selling the fruit. In the past, Father had
always contributed money to the Revolution from
the profits of the ice business and grocery. Even after giving two businesses to the state, Mother intended to continue supporting the Revolution each
year by giving twenty percent of all she earned
from the orchard.

"One day Mother invited a local party cadre to
dinner, and she outlined her plan of support. But
the cadre, an old friend, advised her to uproot the
fruit trees and plant rice instead. Mother was
shocked. It had taken ten years to establish the orchard, and she could not believe he wanted her to
uproot the trees. But the cadre said that the country
needed rice much more than the luxury of fresh
fruit. He warned that her taxes would be increased
considerably, and that the money she made selling
fruit would not be enough to pay taxes, much less
feed her family or contribute twenty percent to the
state. However, he advised, if she cultivated rice,
she could expect much lighter taxes. After years of
experience, Mother felt she knew best how to earn
a living. To clear the fruit trees for rice seemed
preposterous. Mother refused to believe the cadre's
words. It was only later, when a government in-

spector informed her how much tax would be levied on each fruit tree, that Mother understood.

"A great resistance welled up inside her, and, instead of agreeing to clear the trees, she gave the orchard to the government. My grandmother had died, so we no longer had a country refuge. We went to live with an old and dear friend of Mother's in the village whose husband had been sent to a re-education camp. This woman had to sell everything she could in order to support her three children. We were given a room in her house, and Mother made porridge to sell every day at the market.

"There were no men in the house to help support us. Mother and her friend tried to manage, but it was simply impossible to earn enough to feed two adults and five children. Little by little, we sold all our possessions. Each night, we held each other tight and tried desperately to fall asleep and forget our hunger.

"One day, Mr. Bay Nhieu, whom we called Uncle, came to see us. He suggested that we try to escape the country by boat, even though we did not know anyone overseas. Uncle Bay Nhieu was from our village and my parents had helped him many times in the past. His two sons were about to be drafted to fight in Cambodia, where many young men were dying, and he was most anxious to help them escape. Uncle had a boat with provisions ready to go, and two other families were going with him and his sons. They had all contributed money to pay for gasoline, motor oil, and food for the ten days they expected to be at sea. There were still three places on the boat, and he wanted Mother, Bich, and me to join them.

"Mother did not consider herself a political refugee. She only knew that it had become impossible to survive in her own country, and she must leave if her children were to live. She had heard that refugees were often taken aboard foreign ships and resettled in that ship's home country. Just as Uncle Bay Nhieu's sons had no choice, Mother too had no choice but to leave.

"After thinking it over for three days, Mother agreed to go with Uncle Bay. She made arrangements to take Bich and me and follow Uncle into the countryside. I didn't take anything with me. I wore my prettiest blouse, white satin pants frayed at the edges, and a pair of rubber thongs. We walked through the jungle in two groups. The small children were sedated with sleeping pills to keep them them from fussing or crying and possibly alerting the government cadres. We walked nearly two days and nights before reaching the spot where Uncle Bay had hidden the boat.

"As soon as we set sail, we saw four government fishing boats, so we turned back quickly to avoid being seen. The next night, all was clear and we made it away safely. By morning we had reached international waters, and we thought we had reached freedom. Little did we know, this was only the beginning of a nightmare of terror.

"We sailed for just one day before the motor stopped, and we were helplessly tossed about by the waves, unable to control our boat's direction. Everyone prayed that a foreign ship would appear and rescue us, but four days passed with no other ship in sight. We did not even know that we were in the Gulf of Thailand."

Having recounted that much, Hong looked at Dao and asked, "Did your boat meet any foreign ships, elder sister?"

Dao nodded, "Yes, we met a Russian liner, two ships from Panama, an Australian ship, one from Singapore, and one American ship. And when they saw our boat, each of them went right by, as if we were invisible. How could they be so merciless? My mother used to tell me that it brought much merit to be able to save a human life. I'm not sure about merit, but I know it must bring great joy to save another human being. Yet those ships didn't seem to consider us any more important than ants. It was horrible."

Hong responded, "In the beginning, a lot of ships rescued boat people, elder sister. But they found that once they had taken the refugees aboard, no country was willing to accept them, not even temporarily. The refugee camps in Malaysia, Indonesia, and Thailand exist only because the U.N. High Commission on Refugees intervened. These countries actually do not want to let refugees in, and they secretly order their marine police to pull refugee boats back out to sea whenever they can get away with it. Many, many boats are forced to wander on the open sea until they finally sink in a storm. No one knows how many boats have sunk at sea."

Dao's eyes opened wide, "How do you know all this? Have you read these things in a newspaper?"

Hong's eyes filled with sadness. "I know be- cause I know, elder sister. I don't read any newspapers. Singapore is one of the most ruthless ports of all. Some refugees who have arrived in Singapore have sunk their boats to avoid being dragged back out to sea. But after that, many have been arrested and taken somewhere—no one knows where. If a journalist, an embassy, or a U.N. representative knows about them, the government of Singapore cannot mistreat them. In time, the refugees may even be accepted by some Western embassy for immigration to a new country. But if no one knows about them, they will probably remain in prison until they die.

"The Malaysian police often try to intimidate boats by firing at them. Sometimes the bullets seriously damage the boat or wound people aboard. Once, I watched two boats carrying about sixty refugees each, land on Malaysian shore about ten miles north of Mersing. The refugees, including many children, stood on the sand and begged to be allowed in, but the Malaysian police forced them back onto their boats. They cried and pleaded, but the police said they did not have the authority to let them stay. The refugees told the police that their boats were damaged and could not possibly sail again. But the police found someone to repair them.

"Four hours later, they were forced back onto their boats and pushed out to sea. Almost immediately, one of the boats was struck by a huge wave and it capsized. The passengers on the other boat witnessed this tragic scene. Their captain decided to take them back to shore, even at the risk of being shot. They landed and immediately destroyed the boat. The bewildered police decided to house the refugees temporarily in an abandoned barracks. The women and children could not stop crying. The men stared silently into space, refusing to eat or drink even the provisions that the villagers spontaneously brought them.

"Only two men aboard the sunken boat survived. They swam for five hours before being picked up by a Malaysian fishing boat. But when they were brought to shore, they were taken somewhere by the police and never seen again. The police threatened the passengers from the other boat that they would be sent back out to sea on an old boat if they mentioned the incident to anyone. No one knows what happened to those two men. Maybe they were killed to keep the incident hidden from the international press. Not a week passes without an incident like this, elder sister."

Hong spoke as though she had seen it all herself. Dao watched Hong's face become profoundly sad, yet calm. Dao could not explain why, but she believed everything Hong told her, even though it was impossible that a small girl could know so much. But her incredulity was secondary to the pain in her heart. Dao recalled the miseries her own boat had suffered after the engine failed—the thirst, the hunger, the pirates, and all the unspeakably horrible details. But now she was aware of the tragic plight of all her people. How many had perished at sea, she did not dare guess, but she knew it was many, many. Unable to survive in their own homeland, they had fled on boats only to be shot, raped, and robbed, until at last they drowned in the sea. Dao lay her head on Hong's shoulder and wept streams of tears. The sun had set, and the evening wind grew chilly. At last Hong stood up, and holding a cracker and some spring water, offered Dao some nourishment.

Late that night Dao tossed and turned. All she could think of was Dat's boat. Where had the waves carried it? Was there any food or water aboard? If the boat reached Malaysia, would they be allowed to enter a refugee camp, or would the police drag them back out to sea to sink? If Dat died, Dao did not want to live. But then she remembered Hong saying that she must live for her mother and brothers and sisters. Dao whispered, "Dear mother, I will not die. I will live for you and my brothers and sisters." Her tears fell like rain.

Hearing Dao weep, Hong awoke and moved towards her. As if she could feel the sadness in Dao's heart, Hong said, "Many boat people have landed near the refugee camps and been admitted. Don't worry. Though Dat and the others have no more water or food, they will surely be able to hold out for a few more days. And if they meet a kind fisherman, their boat may be pulled to a safe shore."

"But one does not often meet such good fortune. Hong, I'm afraid."

"Don't be. You yourself were thrown overboard by a pirate and yet here you are alive. Strange and wondrous events take place all the time. Just a few months ago, seven young people left Vietnam in a rowboat and rowed all the way to Thailand, where they were admitted to the Songkhla Camp. One family with two young children escaped on a tiny boat, just seven yards long. They were shot at by the authorities as they left the port of Rach Gia. The husband was hit in the chest, but they sailed full speed to escape. He died two days later, but his wife and their two young children struggled for seven days and nights and finally made it to the coast of Thailand. Many sinking boats have been rescued by passing fishermen. The universe is filled with marvels that most of us never see or hear about, elder sister."

Hong continued, "Usually our world revolves around school, shopping, movies, and these kinds of activities. We think these are the most important and real things in the world. But there are many extraordinary and wondrous things hidden throughout the universe. You don't have to go far to seek wonders, they are right in front of us, every day. We need only be aware, and not let our usual preoccupations hide the wondrous universe from us. Don't just dwell on your suffering and miss the brightness in your heart. If your mind is serene, you can see many wonders.

"But enough, it's late and we need to sleep. Tomorrow I will tell the rest of my story. Now I will recite the *Heart of Perfect Understanding Sutra*, and then let us go to sleep. I hope you sleep peacefully."

Hong recited in the way she had heard her grandmother:

> *The Bodhisattva, Avalokita, while moving in the deep course of perfect understanding, shed light on the five skandhas, and found them equally empty. After this penetration, he overcame all pain.*

The soft sounds of her chanting were like raindrops gently falling on flowers. Dao lay quietly and allowed the words of the sutra to fill her heart and mind. Soon she dreamed she saw a refreshing stream of water running through a field dotted with many flowers, yellow and violet.

It was Dao's third day on the island. When she awoke, Hong was already gone. "This little girl certainly likes to do her exploring early," thought Dao. She went to the spring to wash her face and change into the violet blouse from the duffel bag. She washed her other blouse and spread it on the rocks to dry. Though she waited a long time, Hong did not return. Dao took two crackers to eat and some spring water to drink, and then she wandered up the stream hoping to find Hong.

When Dao came to the guava tree she'd discovered the day before, she stopped to pick another fruit. Even though it was still so sour it made her cringe, she relished it. She noticed dandelion greens nearby and she picked a large bunch to take back. A little further upstream she found some chicory and wild watercress, and she picked a handful of each.

Dao returned to the small rock enclosure where she and Hong had spent the night, but Hong had still not returned. Dao thought, "How strange that she disappears every morning!" She called Hong's name over and over until she was hoarse, but there was no answer.

Dao began to worry that Hong had really lost her way this time, as unlikely as that seemed. The more Dao thought about Hong, the more she marveled, "Sometimes when Hong speaks, she sounds like a great master teaching. She comforts me like a mother, and seems to know everything that happens at sea. In fact, she speaks as though she has witnessed it all herself."

Around two in the afternoon, dark clouds gathered and the sky grew turbulent. A great storm was breaking, and Dao crouched beneath the rock ledge picturing Hong somewhere on the island getting drenched like a wet mouse. Her worry grew as the downpour continued. Finally, in the early evening, the rain stopped.

When the sky turned to a dusky violet, Dao's worry increased. Then, at last, Hong returned. She came up from the beach, her hair and clothes again not at all wet, not even a drop. Overjoyed, Dao called her and raced to the beach to hug her as tightly as she could. Hong let Dao hold her for a long time before gently moving out from Dao's arms. Then Hong spoke, "I've got good news, elder sister. Dat's boat has reached shore!"

"What? What did you say? Dat's boat has made it? Really?" Dao asked in a frenzy, not even stopping to wonder how Hong could know such a thing.

"Dat's boat met a Malaysian fishing boat which pulled them to nearby Bidong Island. Everyone was allowed to disembark and enter the refugee camp there. I told you we shouldn't give up hope!"

Dao hastily asked, "Is it really true, little sister? Oh, I'm so happy! Now I'm sure I can go on living! And how is Dat? Was he hurt badly? Are his wounds infected? Is his life in danger?"

Hong shook her head. "Dat is fine. A doctor checked him and all the others. He wasn't hurt badly. Some of the other refugees rinsed his wounds with ginger and water. But he is suffering because he thinks you drowned."

"Oh, Hong, I feel so sorry for him. How can we let him know I'm still alive?"

"There is no way yet, elder sister. When you reach the other shore, you can write him, but we aren't there yet. We just have to wait, I'm not sure how long."

"What if I die on this island and never see him again?"

"There you go again," Hong admonished her, "letting despair take hold of you. You just received wonderful news. Why spoil it with such a terrible thought?"

"I am foolish. Please forgive me. I believe that we will be rescued. But Hong, how did you know about Dat? Where have you been all day? I have been worrying about you."

Hong took Dao's hand gently and led her to some rocks, where they sat down. "I promised to tell the rest of my story today. Every story is both sad and happy. I know you've been wondering how someone as young as I can know so much, even about things that happen far away. Listen, yesterday I said that there are strange and wondrous things that we rarely see or hear, but that does not make them impossible. I am the ten-year-old child Hong. But I am also a fish. . . . You look surprised. Please smile, Dao. . . . Okay, now I can continue telling you the rest of my story.

"After our boat reached international waters, it sailed swiftly for one day. On the second day, our engine failed. Uncle Bay revved the motor again and again, but it just would not start. From then on, our boat was tossed about on the open sea. We did not encounter a single boat for four days. On the sixth day, a storm came up, and we were thrown relentlessly by the wind and the waves. We came so close to capsizing that we dropped all our possessions overboard to lighten the load, even our food and water supplies. By dawn, the storm had calmed, but we were all so exhausted, hungry, and thirsty, that we could not move. As the sun rose, it became hot as an oven, and our parched throats burned without relief. Uncle Bay told us to save our urine to drink, and we did so. At night, the air grew deathly cold. After days of exposure to the elements, most of us became ill.

"My little brother, Bich, got a fever. Without medicine or water, he died the same day. Mother clutched his body in her arms and refused to let go. She wanted to weep, but she had no tears left. All the while, water was seeping in the many holes in our boat. The men took turns bailing it out until they became too weak to continue. Only Uncle Bay had the stamina to keep the boat from capsizing.

"The next day, Uncle Bay told Mother that Bich would have to be buried at sea. She refused, but finally, when his little corpse began to smell, she had to agree. All of us recited the *Heart Sutra*. Then Uncle Bay began to chant the Buddha's name, and the rest of us joined him. As we recited the Buddha's name, Uncle Bay gently removed Bich from Mother's arms, leaned over, laid the child's body on the face of the ocean, and released him. Brother's body quickly sank beneath the waves, and Mother wailed. We chanted the Buddha's name ever more loudly, trying to absorb her tragic cries. When the chanting stopped, Mother collapsed.

"That evening a pirate ship attacked us. They caught our boat with a metal hook and pulled up alongside us. There were twelve of them, armed with sharp knives and clubs. We didn't dare resist. In fact, none of us had the strength to fight back. The pirates robbed what we had left, including any clothes on our bodies worth anything. One pirate approached Mother to see if she had a necklace beneath her blouse. I shouted, 'Don't touch my mother!' but he ignored my cries. He grabbed Mother's blouse and began to rip it open. With all my strength, I hurled myself at him and grabbed his leg to try to make him fall. But I was so weak, he just straightened out his leg and kicked me over the side of the boat. I heard Mother screaming as if possessed by demons, but there was nothing I could do.

"I don't know if it was because of some magical power, but I did not drown. Instead, I found myself swimming and breathing like a fish. After the pirates had grabbed everything they possibly could, they rammed their ship into ours and broke it in two. Water rushed in, but everyone was too weak to move. Heart wrenching cries rose as our boat slowly sank. The pirates revved their engines and sped away.

"I had become a fish about the size of a young girl. But by the time I realized that I could rescue people, Mother and all the others had disappeared. I dove deep to look for Mother, but all I saw was the fathomless water. I swam around that spot for a week, but there was no sign of Mother. Had she been devoured by a shark? Or had she turned into a fish, too? If Mother was a fish, was she nearby looking for me? I resolved to swim the entire Gulf of Thailand searching for Mother.

"Every day I swam quite far, and on full moon nights I returned to the spot where our boat had sunk, in hope of finding Mother. For more than a year, I looked for her every day. Because I swam all over the Gulf of Thailand, I encountered many refugee boats. Whenever I saw a sinking boat, I tried to save at least one person, usually a small child. I carried the child on my back with its head above the water, until we got to a sandy beach. I swam near the coasts of Thailand, Malaysia, and Indonesia, because it was easier to help victims who were already near a shore. Some refugees thought I might be a magic fish, so they followed me. From time to time, I was able to help boats avoid hidden rocks or show them places where there were no police. Other refugees raised their knives to kill and eat me in order to appease their terrible hunger, but when I saw someone draw his knife, I dove deep beneath the water, and the boat lost its guide. I wasn't angry at those who wanted to kill me, because I understood how hungry they were.

"One full moon night in April, I rescued a fourteen-year-old boy and carried him to shore near the port of Kota Baru. I was afraid that the water might carry him back out to sea during the night, so I wiggled up along the sand to push him beyond the water's reach. Then, how marvelous! I turned into a girl again, wearing the same pink shirt, frayed white satin pants, and rubber thongs as before.

"I danced with joy beneath the April moonlight. I called out, 'Ma!' and found that I still had my same voice. Ecstatic, I called out my brother's name, 'Bich!' I chanted the *Heart Sutra* just as my grandmother used to every day. I realized that although I was still a fish, I was also a ten-year-old girl.

"I knew that I was on the coast of Malaysia after crossing the Gulf of Thailand without a boat. I knew I could stay on land, but I wanted to return to the sea to look for my mother and to save children from the sinking refugee boats.

"The boy was not yet conscious, but his chest rose and fell evenly. Confident that he was breathing, I knelt down, kissed him lightly on the forehead, and ran back to the water. When I jumped back into the sea, I became a bright pink fish sparkling in the moonlit water.

"From then on, I went ashore often, either to carry someone to safety, or to mingle with the refugees in the camps to find out about their situations. Everyone assumed I was the daughter of some family in the camp waiting to resettle in another country. But I never stayed in a refugee camp longer than a morning or an afternoon. I spent most of my time looking for Mother and searching for ships to rescue at sea.

"I ate nothing but seaweed and grew very strong. I could swim an entire day without feeling tired and carry a person on my back fifteen nautical miles. The day the pirates attacked your boat, Dao, I was there and saw the whole scene. It was less than two miles from where my own boat had sunk. When you were thrown into the sea, I swam beneath you and carried you towards this island. After pushing you ashore, I went back and discovered that the pirates had left, and that northeasterly winds were blowing your boat towards Trengganu. I hoped that your boat would drift to a fishing area north of Kuala Trengganu, and that one of the fishing boats there would tow your boat to shore in southern Thailand or northern Malaysia, to a place like Patthani, Songkhla, Kota Baru, or Trengganu.

"The next morning, I pushed one of the tins of crackers that had been tossed from the Danish ship all the way to this island. Then I returned to sea and swam that entire day, but there were no other chances to rescue anyone. That evening I carried back a bag of clothing that I found bobbing near the wreckage of a boat destroyed in a bad storm. When I got back to the island, I saw that you were still sleeping, so I opened the clothes bag, wrung out a shirt, and hung it on a branch to dry. The moon had just risen. I sat beside you and placed my hand lightly on your forehead to see if you had a fever, and it was then that you awoke."

Dao grasped Hong's arm to feel that the child before her was a real child of flesh and blood. Hong's clear and innocent eyes looked at Dao as though amused. Dao hugged Hong and cried, "How wondrous, Hong!" The marvelous reality before Dao's eyes was almost too good to be true. And yet, her own joy and gratitude verified the unmistakable wondrousness of Hong's real presence. As if she could read Dao's thoughts, Hong laughed and said, "When you see Dat again, will you see how wondrous he is too? And will you believe he is real?"

Dao felt as if she had awakened from a long sleep. To see Dat again, to hold his hand, would indeed be a miracle. She imagined embracing him and exclaiming, "How wondrous!" just as she had with Hong. Dao remembered how seeing the guava tree the day before had felt like a miracle. She smiled, thinking about how these seemingly ordinary events allowed her to see the world of the present moment in a bright, new way. Suddenly she could even appreciate the small details of her life on this deserted island. Now Hong was telling her that she could continue to live in appreciation of so many precious gifts of the universe.

Dao had spent many hours with Dat, sitting with him, looking into his eyes, being held in his arms, but she had never really thought of him as miraculous. Dao had taken everything in her life for granted—Dat, her family, the sun, the clouds, the trees. . . . Now for the first time she realized how truly wondrous all these things were. Everything was infinitely precious, just like the child Hong sitting before her.

Dao asked Hong more about Dat's boat. Hong explained how she had swum beside the boat until it met a Malaysian fisherman who pulled it to Bidong Island, just beyond the town of Kuala Trengganu. Hong had gone ashore and seen Dat and the others admitted into the camp.

"I am sure a boat will soon pass by here," Hong assured Dao, "and you will be rescued." Before they went to sleep, Hong promised Dao that early the next morning she could watch her dive into the water and turn into a fish.

While morning mist hung in the air, Dao watched Hong go down to the water and wade in up to her chest. She held her palms together, bowed her head, and dived into the water. For an instant, Dao saw the shape of a pink fish waving its tail, creating a froth of bubbles behind it. And then Hong was gone.

Dao looked out over the sea, her heart filled with sadness and love. The ocean had closed over so many of her people, yet beneath that same ocean swam a lone pink fish full of love.

Dao felt sad that Hong would probably never find her mother, and joyful for all Hong had done to help her people. Dao resolved that once she found refuge, she too would work with all her energy to help those in need. Hong had warned Dao about the many hardships that awaited her in the refugee camp, but Dao was not afraid. Knowing that Hong was in the Gulf of Thailand was a great comfort and inspiration to her. Dao would work to overcome difficulties and be worthy of Hong's faith and courage.

All day long Dao sat on the sand knowing Hong was somewhere out at sea. When the sky was twinkling with stars, she heard Hong's voice and saw her friend, luminous in the starlight, stepping along the sand towards her. Overjoyed, Dao stood up to greet Hong. Hong took Dao's hand, and they walked up the island. Dao offered Hong some crackers and spring water. Hong did not eat the crackers but drank the clear water.

Hong recounted her day's discoveries. A refugee boat had sunk near Narathiwat, and among four hundred persons aboard, nearly one hundred had drowned. When Hong arrived, she saw pieces of the boat floating on the waves, including a plank on which was painted the boat's number, "LA1945." One of the surviving passengers described how they had encountered rough seas as soon as they had left Vietnamese waters. Their boat was thrown about for five days and nights. On the sixth night, a huge storm struck, and waves roared against the boat's little cabin and left a gaping hole for water to gush through the hull. Everyone thought their hour of death had come, but thanks to swift hands and an excellent captain, they were able to keep afloat. They struggled that night and all the next day, until around six in the evening they spotted the coast of Thailand and steered the boat towards it. Night descended. The boat could no longer hold them, and their only chance of living lay in their ability to swim to shore. Ninety-seven persons lost their lives. The day dawned on women weeping for their husbands, mothers for their children, brothers for sisters. Grief wailed up and down the beach. Local brigands stole their money and possessions. At last, the Thai police put them on a truck and took them to the refugee camp at Songkhla.

Hong told Dao about a refugee boat that had come to shore near Patthani. It carried only thirty people who had left Vietnam from the port of Ca Mau. Throughout their first two days and nights, they sailed with ease, but on the third day, as they neared Thai waters just twenty miles from Cut Island, they were attacked by pirates disguised as fishermen, who stole their clothing and belongings. The women were all raped twice. After the pirates left, the boat continued to seek a way to shore. The following day the same pirates returned. They checked to make sure that they had not missed anything, and then they raped the women again. Having endured two brutal attacks, the boat people still managed to make it to shore several times but each time they were towed back to sea by marine police.

Two days later, they were attacked by three pirate boats at once. The pirates were furious because there was nothing to steal, so they shot two of the refugee men and threw their bodies into the sea. They threw four others overboard for nearby sharks to attack. Of these, one young man managed to escape. He swam far out, grabbed hold of a barrel that someone had thrown overboard, and then hid behind it. The pirates rammed their vessels against the refugee boat. Four terrified children grabbed floatable plastic containers and jumped into the water. The boat was gashed open, and the pirates left, confident that the boat would soon sink. But the boat did not sink. The children were pulled out of the water, and the boat continued to float on the sea for three more days and nights. During that time, they were attacked twice more by different pirates. These pirates grabbed their few remaining clothes and raped the women, but they did not kill anyone. Finally, on the morning of the next day, the boat was given permission to come ashore, and the police took them to Songkhla. The youngest woman on the boat was sixteen years old. She had been raped twelve times, and appeared to have lost her mind.

Listening to Hong, Dao could not hold back her tears. Who knew how many cruelties were committed each day? Her shoulders shook. She could no longer hold back the flood of anguish inside her. She would never be able to understand how people could be so cruel to one another. Perhaps the end of the world was at hand? She cried for a long time, so long that when she stopped, the moon was shining brightly overhead. She saw Hong sitting quietly beneath the moonlight like a bronze statue. Hong said softly, "I wanted to let you cry so you could ease your pain. Go now and wash your face at the spring. It will refresh you. We can chant the sutra before we sleep. It's already very late and tomorrow I must be off early."

It was Dao's fifth day on the island. She knew it would be dark before Hong returned, and so she did not worry while she waited. She looked out over the sea for any boats that might pass near the island. Following Hong's advice, she tied a shirt onto a stick, so she could run down to the shore and wave it if she spotted a boat. But Dao did not see one boat the entire day.

When Hong returned, she told Dao of the many refugee boats she had seen in the vicinity. Every boat that had neared shore had been threatened by police gunfire, or been tugged back to international waters. Hong encountered one boat with a broken motor floating aimlessly beyond Patthani. There were fifty persons aboard, all dead except for one man who was barely breathing. They had run out of food and water.

Hong also saw a Thai fishing boat pull a refugee boat towards Songkhla. Because the fisherman was afraid of being caught by the police for aiding refugees, he cut the rope that attached the two boats before reaching shore. The refugee boat was trying to make it ashore when a pirate boat came along- side. These pirates took all their jewelry, money, and good clothes, but did not rape any of the women. The refugee boat finally made it to shore, and the refugees were accepted into the Songkhla Refugee Camp.

Hong smiled as she told Dao about a strange boat she had encountered many times in the Gulf. It was a Thai fishing boat called the Shantisuk. Hong noticed all kinds of fishing gear aboard, in- cluding spear guns for large fish, but not once had she seen the eight "fishermen" aboard, including one young woman, do any fishing. Hong had seen them give refugees food, fresh water, gasoline, and sea maps that pointed out dangerous hidden rocks as well as the locations of refugee camps. Hong fol- lowed the Shantisuk once to the port of Patthani. Anchored among the other fishing boats, it did not stand out at all.

Hong admired the quiet mission of this vessel and began paying more attention to it. Though there were only eight people aboard, they spoke to each other in four different languages—Thai, French, English and Vietnamese. Four of them were Vietnamese, three Thai, and one French. Hong swam right beside the boat and floated near the surface in order to hear their conversations.

It appeared that everyone aboard was vegetarian. One morning Hong saw the Vietnamese woman toss back into the water some flying fish that had jumped onto the boat during the night. She also saw the woman release some live fish that she had bought from a small fishing boat near shore. Hong noticed that the woman even spoke to these fish, and she was very moved and felt a special kinship with her. Several times the woman had noticed Hong and called the others to come look at her.

Knowing that these people would not harm her, Hong swam unafraid alongside their boat. By listening to their conversations, she soon understood why their rescue mission had to be carried out in secret. The governments of Thailand, Singapore, Malaysia, and Indonesia did not want to accept refugees on their shores, and they resented any efforts to save refugees at sea. These governments preferred to let refugees die at sea, rather than subject their countries to the economic and political problems of accepting refugees. The Shantisuk had to pose as a fishing boat in order to save people. The Thais aboard, including a young monk from the countryside, disagreed with their country's heartless policy. All eight of them were disciples of a spiritual master who lived in a small hermitage on the mountain peak, Doi Suthep, in northern Thailand.

The Vietnamese aboard the Shantisuk had become citizens of other countries. As Vietnamese nationals, they could not have obtained the necessary documents that would have allowed them to enter Thailand, Malaysia, Singapore, and Indonesia. The French fellow aboard, named Jean Paul, had once been a sailor off the coast of Brittany in France. He could sit in meditation as well as Hong's grandmother, and once Hong had watched him sitting in the full lotus position at the boat's helm.

Hong knew they kept many dried foods aboard, including packets of instant noodles, of which Jean Paul was especially fond. Even though the Shantisuk was disguised as a fishing boat, it had been attacked once by pirates in Thai waters. The pirate vessel was equipped with radar and could travel at great speed with an eight hundred horsepower engine. They threatened those aboard at gunpoint and took their money and food supplies. They did not search for jewelry or gold, as they knew it was not a refugee boat, and they left the men and the woman unharmed. Everyone sat quietly and let the pirates take whatever they wanted.

After this attack, Captain Luc suggested that they buy a gun for self-defense. This stirred a debate which lasted several days and nights. Hong listened and understood their difficult situation. Luc's suggestion was rejected by several aboard. As disciples of a pacifist monk, they did not want to use weapons to protect themselves. But Luc said, "Having a gun does not mean we are going to kill anyone." In the past, Luc had been a good marksman, and he felt sure they could use a gun to fire into the air or hit something small on the pirates' boat in order to scare off the pirates. The woman aboard smiled and remarked that it was only when one's spirit was weak that one thought about guns. If their motivation was to help people, they would be protected. "Before we left the mountain," she said, "Master told us we must respect the sacredness of life and use only love to respond to hatred and violence. He told us we were not to harm even a fish in the sea."

Luc countered, "A gun is only an outer form. The essential thing is how we use it. We could use the gun in a completely nonviolent way. I'm sure the Master would agree with me."

In the midst of these debates, however, their most pressing concern was that they had been discovered by pirates to be foreign fishermen. The pirates were from Mahachai, located in the Samu Sakorn district, a place of ill repute much like Cau Muoi in Vietnam.

"If the Mahachai pirates wish to harass us, we will not be able to go on with our project. We are all grown people, and we have to make our own decisions. We cannot go running back to the mountain with every problem to ask the Master's advice," said Luc. And so the discussion continued.

For some time after that, Hong did not encounter the Shantisuk. But just the day before, Hong had seen it near the northern shore of Malaysia, and heard several things about their dealings with pirates that were most heartening. In Mahachai, Luc had managed to make friends with the leader of the pirates who had attacked them—a man named Tana, or Tan for short. Tan, accomplished in the martial arts, had accepted Luc as a brother, praising his bravery and skill.

Luc had gone on his own into Mahachai to seek out Tan. Tan's followers were taken aback by the grim expression of resolve on Luc's face as he approached Tan, especially after Luc threw one of them to the ground when he tried to bar his path. When Luc demanded Tan's whereabouts, several pirates jumped up to warn Tan of his arrival. Tan invited Luc into his home and asked him to sit down. Then suddenly, Tan struck at Luc with a karate blow. Luc reacted quickly, moving out of the way to avoid being struck, and then calmly sat back down. Tan grabbed a sharp knife from the table and made a menacing stab at Luc. Luc did not try to grab the knife but only leaned far enough to avoid Tan's thrust. After a second thrust, Tan did not test Luc anymore but accepted him as a brother.

Tan was in need of a good marksman and invited Luc to join his band of pirates. He also promised he would order his followers to return everything they had stolen from the Shantisuk. Tan still believed that Luc's boat was only a fishing vessel. He suggested Luc sell the Shantisuk and become the captain of an eight hundred horsepower boat equipped with radar.

Luc did not dare reject Tan's offer outright, but answered that he needed some time to think it over and discuss it with his friends. Luc also said he needed a gun for self-defense against the pirates. Tan said he knew some police and could arrange to provide Luc with a gun permit. How strange, thought Luc, that Tan should have so much authority. Luc got the permit within an hour, but because his friends still refused to have a gun aboard the Shantisuk, he did not buy one.

Luc's boat was not harassed again by Tan's men, but other pirates still posed a threat, among them a group based in Trad. The Shantisuk's policy, the wisest one possible in Hong's mind, was to race away full speed whenever they encountered a pirate vessel. But those aboard feared that many of the pirate vessels had radar and guns, and could travel much faster. Before there had been refugees in the area, pirates had attacked Malaysian and Thai fishing boats, sometimes killing the fishermen aboard after robbing them. The Thai marine police had often sent out patrols, but were unable to destroy the pirates' hold. Recently, an entire patrol led by a Thai police captain had been killed by pirates near Ko Kut Island—the same location where the Shantisuk had almost been robbed.

Having set sail from Trad one night, the Shantisuk navigated towards Ko Chang and Ko Kut Islands when they spotted two vessels. Thanks to Luc's keen observation, he guessed their ill intentions when they were still five hundred yards away. The channel was quite narrow and they knew they could not possibly avoid the pirates if they continued on course. Jean Paul observed that the boats signalled one another by flashing lights, even though there was still enough daylight to see. In order to find out whether they were pirates or not, Luc steered towards the right to see what they would do. After exchanging another flashing light signal, the two boats veered to the right as well, in order to block the Shantisuk. Hong, who was close by, began to worry. Suddenly, Shantisuk veered around and fled full speed back towards Trad, where many other boats were still anchored. At three in the morning, Shantisuk set sail with a host of other fishing boats to avoid being attacked.

From then on, Shantisuk no longer sailed around Trad.

For some time now pirates had been doing whatever they pleased and no one could control them. Word had spread like wildfire when pirates first found gold on the refugee boats. Soon pirates had staked out territories at sea where they could attack refugee boats, especially in the vicinity of Ko Kut and Ko Chang, where the greatest number of refugee boats passed. Every day, the numbers of pirates increased, due to poverty and hardship. Many were not "professionals," in that they did not own guns, but instead carried knives, hammers, and clubs. The Thai authorities were aware of the pirates' activities, but because they did not want any more refugees to come ashore, they ignored the cruel goings-on. Yet even if the authorities had wanted to control the piracy, it was unlikely they could have done so.

One day when the Shantisuk was docked at Chanthaburi, a Thai man approached Luc and suggested they use the dinghy to search for gold at sea. When Luc asked where gold was to be found, the fellow replied he knew of some buried on a small island near Ko Kut. After questioning him carefully, Luc learned that the man was the sole survivor of a band of eighteen pirates who had robbed four refugee boats near Ko Kut and buried the bounty on a nearby small island. Soon after, they were attacked by another band of pirates for crossing into their territory, and they all had been killed except for him. Now he wanted Luc to accompany him to the island to claim the gold. Luc refused, saying he did not have the courage. Hong knew that the real reason was that Luc had not come to the Gulf of Thailand for gold.

Hong told Dao that the refugees' greatest danger was the pirates. Piracy had grown so widespread that nearly every refugee boat was attacked at least once. Some had been attacked more than ten times. The average was three or four. Some pirates were ruthlessly savage. Others pitied the refugees after robbing them, and agreed to pull them closer to shore. Some pirates, after robbing and raping the boat people, killed everyone aboard and sank the boat. Others only took money and clothes, but did not touch the women.

Dao trembled as she listened to Hong. She felt her courage seep away. But Hong assured her she would seek every means possible to help Dao get to the other shore without encountering any more pirates. That night Dao asked Hong to teach her the *Heart of Perfect Understanding Sutra.* She knew the sutra would help her find serenity and strengthen her spirit. Sad for her fate and for the fate of all her people, Dao's tears fell even in her sleep.

When she awoke, Dao knew that Hong had already gone to sea. She walked to the spring to wash, and then ate one cracker to ease her hunger and drank more spring water. Dao climbed up on a large boulder in the shade and tried to sit in meditation. She had never meditated before, but she imitated the cross-legged position and kept her back straight. She had once heard someone say that breathing was the most important part of meditation, so she began to take long and quiet breaths, relaxing her face in a slight smile. After fifteen minutes, Dao felt relaxed and refreshed, and quite stable both physically and spiritually.

Dao began to recite the *Heart Sutra*. After chanting it several times, she smiled when she realized she was imitating Hong's voice. She did not understand the meaning of the sutra's words, but their sounds were joyous and comforting. She was especially struck by one section:

> *Hear, Shariputra, all dharmas are marked with emptiness; they are neither produced nor destroyed, neither defiled nor immaculate, neither increasing nor decreasing. Therefore, in emptiness there is neither form, nor feeling, nor perception, nor mental formations, nor consciousness.*

It seemed to her that if she repeated this a thousand times, she might understand the deep meaning of the sutra.

These words were at once as gentle as floating clouds and as explosive as thunder. Dao knew they contained something very important, though she could not penetrate their meaning. At the same time, she knew she understood something, though she was not sure exactly what. She only knew that she was drawn to those words.

Dao stopped chanting, when she saw that Hong had returned much earlier than usual. The sun was poised straight above. Dao ran to meet Hong, and she led her to a shady place while she ran to fetch some water. After drinking, Hong looked at Dao and said:

"Elder sister, get ready to cross to the other shore this afternoon."

Before Dao could ask anything, Hong continued, "A refugee boat will pass by here in about
three hours. You have plenty of time to get ready.
Take all the crackers and the duffel bag of clothes.
When the boat approaches, tell them to come
ashore to refill their water containers. I'll catch
their attention to be sure they see you and come to
pick you up."

Dao grasped Hong's arm. "Will you come with
me? I'm so afraid."

Hong smiled and said, "Why should I cross to
the other side? I need to remain here. I must continue looking for my mother and helping refugees
in trouble. Today is the Thai New Year and everyone is at home celebrating. There isn't a pirate
vessel in sight, not even a fishing boat. Let's go
down to the beach and I'll trace in the sand the
route from here to Ko Kut Island, from Ko Kut to Ko
Chang Island, and from Ko Chang Island to the
Leam Sing district in the province of Chanthaburi.
The local villagers in that area take refugees
ashore and give them food, water and medicine. By
tomorrow the police will escort you and the others
to the Leam Sing refugee camp."

Hong led Dao down to the beach. With her finger, she traced in the sand a map of the Gulf of
Thailand, explaining every detail to Dao. Hong
carefully pointed out the spots where hidden rocks
lay, and she warned Dao how to look carefully at
the sea surface and veer away from places where
the waves indicated the presence of large, sub-
merged rocks. Hong taught Dao how to tell directions by the sun and the stars, and by the locations
of Ko Kut and Ko Chang Islands. Then she erased

the map and asked Dao to draw it, saying aloud all that Hong had told her. Hong repeated all the things that Dao had not yet fully grasped.

When they were finished, she asked Dao, "Do you know anyone in Europe, Australia, or America?"

"Yes, I have an uncle in France."

Hong advised, "When you get into Leam Sing Camp, write a letter to your uncle immediately. Ask the Reverend Doug Kellum, who visits Leam Sing Camp every week and helps the refugees, to mail it for you in Chanthaburi. Ask your uncle to send a telegram to Dat at the Pulau Bidong Refugee Camp in Malaysia, just off the coast from Kuala Trengganu, telling him you are still alive and in the Leam Sing Camp. You can also write a letter directly to Dat yourself. Tell the U.N. representative that you have an uncle in France and that you want to file a request to be resettled there. Dat plans to request to go to France as well, doesn't he? Remind him he needs to request specifically to go to France. And when you get to the camp, please don't forget to make sure you are seen by a doctor. Tell him privately you do not want any scars from the pirates remaining in your body or your spirit."

Looking up, Dao saw two shining tears in Hong's eyes. She hugged Hong tightly. "I'll do just as you say, little sister. Will I ever see you again?"

Moving gently from Dao's arms, Hong led Dao to sit on a boulder in the cool shade. She said, "I might have a chance to see you again, but I'm not sure. So for now, let's consider this our last afternoon together. Listen, elder sister, refugees are now coming out in such great numbers that all the neighboring countries have agreed to take strong measures to refuse them entry. They are carefully policing their beaches to prevent refugees from coming ashore. But that's not all. They are also planning to organize anti-refugee demonstrations to support their practice of forcing refugees back on boats and towing them out to international waters. If they carry out such a plan, our people will all die. I hope that international opinion will prevent it. But once you get to the refugee camp, you must warn our people so they can prepare to defend themselves. Work together and devise ways to prevent such actions from taking place. Even at night, you must be on guard and ready to resist. If you are ordered back onto your boat, refuse to do so, even if they thrust their guns at your chest. In the event you see they mean to carry out their threats of violence, you must find some way to sink or destroy all the boats remaining on shore outside the refugee camp.

"Life in the refugee camp you are about to enter is very difficult, just as in the other camps of Songkhla, Pulau Bidong, Pulau Tengah, Pulau Pinang and many others in this region. You will have to remain there for four, six, or even eight months. If you can, elder sister, as a special favor to me, please give all your energy to those people suffering in the camp."

Hong looked up and laughed, though her eyes were still moist with tears. "I have some good news. Captain Luc went to meet Tan again, and this time he told Tan the whole truth about the Shantisuk. He said, 'Knights never oppress others. You might temporarily steal gold from the rich to help those who are hungry, but you never have the right to kill or rape. Your followers must never sully your good name.' Luc was very courageous, and Tan promised he would give such an order to his followers.

"But elder sister, there are hundreds of pirate bands on the sea. Perhaps the few followers of Tan won't threaten the lives and welfare of refugees, but what about all the others? The Shantisuk itself is being threatened by other bands of pirates. I'm afraid that one day soon they will not be able to sail anymore. I'm afraid for their lives. Perhaps the Master on Doi Suthep mountain will call them back because of the dangers at sea. But, look, in the distance, your boat is approaching! Get the branch with the shirt and we'll go down to the shore."

On the eastern horizon, Dao saw a black dot. Each minute it grew larger until finally she could see clearly that it was a refugee boat. Hong said, "Wait for them to come a little closer and then wave the shirt. Don't tell anyone aboard about me, okay? I'll swim out and catch their attention so that they see your signal for help. Remember, do as I've told you, and especially remember to destroy your boat as soon as you get to shore."

Hong hugged Dao tightly. Then, just like a child, she let go of Dao and ran towards the water. She dove into the sea and swam out until Dao could no longer see her. Dao waved the shirt on the stick back and forth. She walked forward until the water rose up to her knees, all the while waving her flag. The boat saw her signal, and the pilot altered his course, steering in the direction of the island.

The Moon Bamboo

The Moon Bamboo

It was late afternoon by the time Mia finished gathering the last bundle of bamboo shoots. She lifted it to her shoulder and walked along the path leading out of the bamboo grove. Her two cousins, Chanh and Cam, sat beneath a banyan tree on the hill, leisurely combing each other's hair as they waited for Mia. When they finally saw her coming, they dusted off their clothes, lifted their own bundles onto their shoulders, and joined Mia for the walk home.

Since early that morning, Mia had worked very hard. Chanh and Cam had picked just a few shoots when they abandoned their work for the cool shade of the tree. Mia, careful to choose only the youngest, most tender shoots, finished filling her cousins' bundles before filling her own. She knew that she would be beaten by her aunt if she picked any shoots that were not tender and sweet.

From the day Mia was orphaned and taken in by her mother's sister, she had endured abuse and cruelty. Because Mia was more beautiful than her older cousins, they were jealous of her and always managed to get her into trouble with their mother, even though she usually did their work for them.

When the three girls reached a grove of sim trees bordering a spring, they put down their bundles and rested. Chanh declared that she was hungry and wanted a piece of sim fruit. The girls gaily picked some fruit, and lay on the grass enjoying its sweet-and-sour taste. Before long, the moon rose in the sky, and Mia urged her cousins to return home, but they ignored her. Cam wanted to swim in the cool spring, so the three girls undressed and plunged into the refreshing water, giggling and shouting as they splashed each other.

Suddenly, Mia heard the sound of someone softly clearing his throat. She turned around but saw no one. Certain that the sound had come from a man and not from either of her cousins, she looked up and was startled to see on the moon a young farmer leaning on his hoe, looking down and smiling at her. Mia felt extremely embarrassed, and she dunked down into the water, as Chanh and Cam continued to play, unaware of the observer. When some passing clouds covered the moon, Mia ran out of the water and hurriedly put on her clothes. Chanh and Cam, thinking that Mia no longer wanted to swim, called, "Come on, Mia! Swim some more! Why are you in such a rush to get home?"

Without responding, Mia lifted her head. The soft, radiant light of the moon shone through the parting clouds, and the three girls all saw the young farmer. But he was not looking at Chanh or Cam. His gaze was only for Mia, who was trying to hide beneath the leafy branches of a tree. Her cousins resented the special attention Mia was receiving, and they did all they could to distract the young man, to no avail. A moment later, dense clouds covered the moon again, and the two cousins, angry and disappointed, climbed onto the bank, got dressed, and picked up their bamboo shoots. On the way home, neither Chanh nor Cam spoke one word to Mia. That night the moon did not show its face again.

Mia's aunt scolded her for returning home so late and for picking such tough bamboo. In fact, all the bamboo she had picked was tender and young, perfect for eating. The tough bamboo shoots had been picked by her negligent cousins. But they feigned ignorance and Mia took the blame. Of course, returning late had not been Mia's idea either, as they well knew. More than likely, Mia's aunt also realized this, but she had fallen into the habit of blaming Mia for all her own troubles.

The next evening the villagers organized a full moon celebration, but Mia was not allowed to go. As a ploy to keep Mia from getting all the attention from the fellow on the moon, Chanh and Cam told their mother that Mia should remain at home to guard the pigs from thieves. They also hid Mia's one decent set of clothes in the rice barrel, for they knew that she would not dare to venture out in her tattered house clothes.

The steady beat of the village drums sounded all night, echoing Mia's own anxious heartbeat. There were so few full moon celebrations in a year, so few nights of song and dance, and she could not be there to share in the fun. To ease her disappointment, Mia gazed at the moon from the porch. Without a cloud in sight, the moon shone brilliantly. But tonight there was no sign of the young farmer hoeing his fields. Didn't he know a celebration was taking place on earth? The bright moonlight and the steady pounding of the drums made Mia's disappointment unbearable. She resolved she would attend the celebration despite her aunt's orders. But when she went inside to change, she could not find her good clothes anywhere. She knew her cousins must have hidden them. In vain, she searched everywhere and then she sat down to reflect on her situation.

She thought about how her aunt and cousins had treated her the past few years. She remembered the times that she had gone hungry, the beatings and cursings she had endured. Chanh and Cam had a new set of clothes sewn every year. Mia had not had anything new for three years, and now even her one very worn set of nice clothes had been hidden. The more she thought about her situation, the more resentment flooded her heart. "How can they be so cruel?" she thought. "I never do them any harm, and they always hurt me." So she decided to run away. Taking only her personal knife, she stepped outside and latched the door behind her. Alone, she entered the forest to start a new life.

Late that night when Chanh, Cam, and the aunt returned home, they could not find Mia anywhere. They guessed that she had sneaked out to the full moon celebration even in her tattered clothes, and the aunt declared that she would beat Mia in the morning for daring to disobey her. But Mia did not return the next day. Chanh had to carry the water from the well, do all the cooking, and sweep the house. Cam had to gather duckweed from the marsh and cook bran porridge for the pigs. They cursed Mia as they worked. If Mia had been there, they would never have dirtied their hands with such tasks. Several days passed, and still there was no sign of Mia. They knew she had run away. Without Mia, housework came to a standstill, and her aunt and cousins realized how much they depended on her. Chanh and Cam were only willing to do the most basic tasks, such as carrying water from the well and cooking meals. They neglected all other chores such as straightening the house, sweeping and scrubbing, tending the garden, and feeding the livestock. News of Mia's disappearance spread quickly. The villagers knew very well it was because of the cruel way she had been treated by her aunt.

In the village there was a young fellow named Tao, who was both kind and industrious. He was in love with Mia, and his mother had asked her aunt for Mia's hand in marriage to her son. But the aunt had replied that she had to find husbands for Chanh and Cam first. She suggested that Tao marry Chanh, but he flatly refused. Mia knew about all of this. She knew Tao loved her, and it was true that she had feelings for him. But she had not yet given much thought to marriage.

One morning, Tao went by the aunt's house to inquire about Mia's disappearance, and he found the aunt hiring men to search for Mia in the forest. Carrying bows and arrows and long knives, they looked more prepared to go on a hunt for wild animals than to seek a young girl. Tao joined them, but after three days of searching, they found no sign of Mia. They concluded she had been swallowed alive by a boa constrictor or devoured by a tiger, bones and all. Tao returned home with a heavy heart. He could not eat for three days.

Of course, the aunt's regrets were no more than the regrets one might feel in losing an excellent maid. Seeing the demise of her household, she began to scold and scream at Chanh and Cam, and the atmosphere in their home grew increasingly unbearable.

❋ ❋ ❋

One day while gathering wild figs in the forest, Mia heard a group of men approaching. She quickly looked for a place to hide and found a hollow in a tree just large enough for her. As she sat concealed from view, she listened to the men's conversation and learned they had been hired by her aunt to find her. She knew that if she were returned to her aunt, she would surely be beaten. She sat perfectly still.

After a moment, one fellow said, "We've looked everywhere. Most likely she's been eaten by a tiger. Let's return home." Mia waited until the men were far out of reach before she dared breathe normally again. Cautiously, she climbed out of the tree, shuddering about what might have happened if they had found her.

Mia knew that from that time on, no one would look for her again. Relieved, she cut leaves and branches and built a small hut. She knew the forest well and had no difficulty finding edible fruits and wild greens to eat. She was fortunate not to encounter any poisonous snakes. She often met rabbits and deer, but she had no desire to hunt them for food.

One day while gathering bamboo shoots, Mia came across a tender pink shoot, smooth as agate and fragrant as magnolia and orange blossoms. Using her knife, she dug up the young plant, careful not to damage the roots, and gently carried it back to plant by her hut. Mia watered the sprout every day and was delighted to see how quickly it grew into a firm bamboo tree with an emerald green trunk and smooth, shiny leaves. She continued to tend it affectionately and, before long, the young bamboo tree had grown three times higher than the roof of her hut.

One night it was too hot and humid to sleep. Mia decided to refresh herself by bathing in a cool stream nearby. Moonlight illuminated the forest. Splashing herself, Mia remembered the night long ago when she and her cousins had paused to swim. Mia lifted her face to the moon and gasped when she saw the young farmer hoeing his fields. He looked down and smiled at her.

Shy and embarrassed, Mia sank beneath the water, leaving only her nose and eyes peeking above the surface. A moment later, clouds drifted by and covered the moon. Mia dashed from the water, dressed, and ran back to the hut. The moon did not reveal itself again that night. Black clouds tumbled across the sky and a great storm broke. All night the rains pounded.

When the first rays of dawn appeared, Mia was awakened by the sound of rushing water overflowing the stream's banks. Water poured down from the mountain and rushed around Mia's hut. The wind howled. When Mia looked outside, all she could see was the flash of white water. She did not know what to do to save herself. Water rushed into the hut and rose to her ankles and then to her knees. Panic-stricken, she ran outside and clung to the bamboo tree.

She began to climb the tree. When she was high as the roof of her hut, Mia looked out over the forest. All she could see was a great curtain of silver rain. As the flood waters rose, she climbed even higher, her arms and legs clinging to the bamboo tree. The tree stood straight and solid as the rising waters dashed against it. Continuing up, Mia soon found herself higher than the highest trees in the forest. It began to feel as if the bamboo tree itself was also stretching upwards, its green leaves appearing and disappearing in the torrents of rain.

A mighty gust of wind came up and caused the bamboo to lean all the way over to Mia's old village, until it poised exactly above her aunt's house. Mia looked at the house, set among areca trees which were shaking wildly in the wind, and knew she could jump down onto the roof if she wished. But she had not forgotten the years of abuse she suffered at the hands of her aunt and cousins. She hesitated. Should she jump to safety? No, she would rather die than return to her old life. At that moment, the bamboo righted itself and stretched all the way to the moon. When she saw the moon's surface only a few yards away, Mia summoned her remaining strength and climbed the last bit of tree. She reached out and placed her foot upon the moon.

The moon's unfamiliar surface seemed enormous. The rocks, soil, and sand were golden yellow, unlike the brown, red, and black hues Mia knew on earth. She saw before her fields of a curious sort of rice, odd vegetable gardens, and small villages in the distance. The houses had many windows and were more solidly constructed than the thatch and palm leaf homes Mia knew.

Hearing a bird sing, Mia looked up. She had never seen such a bird before! And the branch on which it perched was unlike any branch she knew. Mia was met by one surprise after another. She followed a path that wound alongside a field and discovered it led to a small and tidy house. She hesitated before the gate.

Mia was startled by the familiar sound of a man softly clearing his throat. She turned around, and there before her stood the very young farmer she had seen while she bathed in pools on earth. His hoe was propped over his shoulder, and he smiled like someone who had just discovered gold. Mia felt too timid to speak, but she knew she could not just stand there. After all, she had made the decision herself to come to the moon. Taking a breath to calm herself, she asked, "Is this your home?"

The young farmer nodded. "And are you an earth woman who has just arrived on the moon?"

His language was foreign to her ears, yet somehow Mia understood him. She nodded and said, "There was a flood on earth, so I climbed up here. I'll return home after a few days."

The young man invited Mia into his home and brought her a refreshing drink. They sat and talked for a long time. Mia learned that his name was Dan and he lived alone. His parents had both passed away, and his two younger sisters were married and living in distant villages. Dan owned and tended several acres of land which grew a strange, rice-like grain, a kind of sweet potato, and fruit trees. He tended all his land by himself.

Shyly, Mia said, "This isn't the first time I've seen you."

Dan smiled. "And this isn't the first time I've seen you. The first time was when you were out gathering bamboo shoots with two other girls. The three of you swam in a spring. Then I saw you again, alone in the forest, several times—building a hut, tending a young bamboo tree, gathering wild fruits and greens. I saw you again last night, bathing alone."

Mia remembered the night before when the moon had shone brightly. She lowered her head. Seeing her tattered clothes, she felt ashamed, and placed her hand over the tears in the cloth which revealed her skin.

Dan said gently, "Please don't worry about that, Miss Mia." He went into the back room and offered her a set of clothes that had belonged to his youngest sister. Mia hesitated, but then accepted them. Dan showed her to the bedroom and left her there alone, closing the door behind him. Mia removed her old clothes, still damp from the rain. She held up the strange clothes Dan had given her. Only after several attempts did she figure out the proper way to wear them.

She stepped outside and asked Dan if she could wash her own clothes so that when she returned to earth she could return his sister's things. Dan led her to a clear stream and waited as she rinsed out her old clothes. Together they returned to his house, and he prepared a meal for her. He served the food on an unusual platter without any chopsticks. Mia felt very awkward as she watched Dan in order to learn how to eat the food.

After dinner, Dan asked her about her life on earth, and he listened intently while she told him everything. Learning about her situation, the affection and love he already felt for her grew deeper. When she had finished speaking, he asked her if she would become his wife. "Together we could tend these acres of land, Mia. There's plenty to eat here. Why should you return to earth where your aunt and cousins only abuse you? You cannot live forever in the forest eating fruit and wild greens. Eventually you will grow ill and die."

Mia thought about it for just a short while. "Yes," she decided, "I will become your wife."

Mia learned Dan's language and before long she could converse fluently with her husband and the other villagers. She quickly learned how to tend the fields on the moon. In no time at all, the two of them created a happy and secure life together. Mia gave birth to two children. She named her first-born son Summer, and her daughter Spring, after the seasons of their birth.

One day Mia's aunt wandered deep into the forest with her two daughters to gather bamboo shoots. By chance, she discovered an abandoned hut and immediately guessed it had belonged to Mia, and that she might still be alive. When she saw the bamboo tree rising to the moon, she was certain

Mia had climbed to the moon and was now living there. She wanted to go up herself to persuade Mia to return, but she was far too stout to make such a climb, and her two daughters were too frail and lazy.

It was early in the morning and the moon had not yet set. Looking up at the white globe, Mia's aunt could barely discern the uppermost leaves of the bamboo tree fluttering against the moon's surface. Looking even more carefully, she suddenly caught a vague glimpse of Mia working among the fields on the moon. "She's still an industrious worker," thought the aunt. "Since the day she left, I've realized what an asset she was." The aunt plotted how she could entice Mia to return to earth. She called her daughters to walk home, and a sinister smile formed on her lips as she went over the plan in her mind.

The following day when the aunt went to market, she informed all her friends that any fellow who could climb to the moon and bring back Mia could have her for his wife. By evening, all the young men in the surrounding villages had heard about the offer. There were many young men who had hoped to marry Mia, but who had been thwarted because the aunt had wished to find husbands for Chanh and Cam first. This was their chance. They gathered at the aunt's house, sixteen in all. Among them was the kind and attractive Tao.

The aunt led them to the bamboo tree in the forest next to Mia's hut, which now leaned over to one side and was missing most of its thatch. The bamboo tree, however, still stood straight and tall, its trunk glistening like emerald and its uppermost leaves piercing the clouds.

"How can we be sure this bamboo tree really reaches all the way to the moon?" asked one fellow. It was a cloudy day and no one could see the moon.

The aunt replied, "Believe me, I saw Mia with my own eyes working in a rice field up there. Whoever makes it to the moon, tell Mia how much I miss her. Tell her that if she returns, I will always love her and never beat her or yell at her again."

The first fellow nodded and grabbed hold of the tree to begin his climb. But the bamboo trunk was unusually smooth and the branches were far apart. He climbed only five or six lengths before he slipped straight back down. Undaunted, he spat on his hands and made a second attempt. But still he could make no progress.

The others, anxious to prove their strength, met with no better success, even though they each tried two or three times. When it was Tao's turn, he gave his best effort, but like all the others, he came right back down the slippery trunk. One fellow, growing suspicious, asked aloud, "That bamboo is so smooth, how could Mia ever have made it to the moon?" Tao had been asking himself the same question. Most of them suspected that Mia had never climbed to the moon. They thought this whole event must have been a scheme by the aunt to make them forget Mia once and for all and turn their attentions to Chanh and Cam. Angry and disgusted, they left, swearing they would never speak to the conniving aunt again.

But Tao truly believed that Mia had gone to the moon. He left with the others, but he returned to Mia's abandoned hut early the next morning, determined to climb the bamboo tree. He brought with him a sharp knife and a gourd filled with fresh water, and he began to climb up as far as he could without slipping. Then he took out his knife and cut a small notch in the tree, just large enough to provide a grip for his foot. It worked! He cut more notches, and as he ascended higher and higher, the cuts he had made below were already healing on the amazingly healthy tree. By noon, he had climbed more than half a mile. He reached for the gourd and took a long drink to quench his thirst. He knew he had to ration his water wisely, because he still had a long way to climb. He continued up carefully, stopping occasionally to catch his breath. He no longer dared look below, for fear the height would make him dizzy. In this way, Tao climbed for two days and two nights.

On the morning of the third day, when the sun had just risen, Tao heard a bird singing above his head. He looked up and saw that the moon was no more than ten yards away. Bamboo leaves fluttered above him and he felt a sudden surge of strength. In the space of just three breaths, Tao was on the moon. Clinging to a bamboo branch, he lowered his feet to the surface.

Because his climb had been far more arduous than Mia's, Tao did not notice much of the moon scenery. He simply followed the path before him. It was, of course, the very path that led to Dan's house. When he reached the house, there was no one in sight. After waiting a while to see if someone would appear, Tao walked out into the fields, and suddenly, he caught sight of Mia working in a patch of what appeared to be melons. He hid behind some bushes, cupped his hands around his mouth, and made a cry like the cuckoo bird.

Mia was startled. She stopped what she was doing and stared straight ahead. For five years, she had not heard that familiar sound. Excitedly, she began to search for the bird. Tao made another call and Mia found him. He stood up to greet her. It was the first time she had seen someone from earth since she had arrived, and here was the very earth person for whom she had always felt the most affection. Overjoyed, she asked Tao when he had arrived. They sat and talked on the edge of the rice field, and Mia told him how homesick the cuckoo's call had made her feel.

After a long conversation, Tao learned that Mia was already married. His heart sank, but he made a great effort not to show his disappointment. He asked Mia about life on the moon, about moon customs, clothes, and food. In turn, Mia asked Tao how life had been on earth.

"During these past years, there have not been any more floods. The harvests have been plentiful. You should return to earth to live, Mia. Life here is too strange. Surely you cannot be truly happy."

"Am I happy?" Mia asked herself. For five years she had lived in peace. Kind and gentle Dan had never spoken an angry word to her. They had prospered by their hard work, and had never known want or hunger. Summer, her four-year-old son, and Spring, her three-year-old daughter, were darling, bright children. She had only to recall what life had been like with her aunt to know that her moon life was indeed a happier one. She answered, "Tao, I've found peace here. I cannot return to earth. If I did, I would surely encounter my aunt again, and I suffered enough with that family. Besides, I have a husband and children here. How could I ever leave them to return to the earth?"

Knowing he could not persuade Mia to abandon her life on the moon, Tao talked instead about earth activities. He described the cheerful days when young men and women sang songs back and forth as they harvested the rice. He described how they gathered on the village courtyard at evening to thresh the rice beneath the golden harvest moon, while carrying on lively, flirtatious conversations. Mia's eyes grew bright.

Seeing her homesickness grow, Tao continued to describe other familiar scenes on earth—swimming in the fresh, cool springs; mornings spent gathering sim fruit; full moon nights of song and dance; the first warm days of spring gathering the plum and peach blossoms that perfumed the mountain forests. He reminded her of special foods like the New Year's earthcakes, sweet rice with mung beans, steamed coconut cakes, candied tamarind, stewed bananas, red beans with rice dumplings and coconut milk, salted fish stewed with greens, sour soup, sweet mung bean soup. The mention of these made Mia's mouth water. It had been such a long time since she had enjoyed their tastes.

"You don't wish to return to live on earth, and I won't try to persuade you," said Tao. "But why don't you come to visit for a few days?"

Mia's eyes shined at the idea. She thought there could be no harm if she went for just a brief visit. Dan had taken the children to their aunt's, and they would not be home until nightfall. Mia answered, "A few days would be too long, my friend. It would never do for my husband and children to return home and find me gone. I will come only for the afternoon. I must return here by nightfall."

Mia recalled from that day long ago that climbing to the moon takes about three hours. She did not realize that the tree had sprung up at a terrific speed while she herself climbed only a few yards. Tao knew that the slide down would be quick enough, but that climbing back up might take more than two days and nights. But he said nothing. His only thought was to find a way to get Mia back to earth.

They walked together to the bamboo tree. Tao told Mia to grab hold of a branch, wrap her legs around the tree, and slide down. Mia did as she was told and slid rather quickly. Tao waited until she had gone a good distance, and then he grabbed hold of the tree. In his right hand he held his knife. Every few feet, he reached up and cut off a section of bamboo, which fell randomly to earth below, without Mia's notice. When she finally reached the earth, the sun was directly overhead. She let go of the tree and saw her old hut, now in ruins.

Mia was still looking around when Tao arrived. He said, "If we return to your old hamlet, we may meet your aunt. Let's go instead to the highland village. No one there knows you." So they walked together in the direction of the highland village.

Mia was delighted to see jackfruit, bananas, sandalwood, and other trees she knew so well. As they emerged from the other side of the forest, she felt a great joy walking alongside fields of sweet potatoes and green rice. This marvelous earth was Mia's own homeland. A grasshopper jumped near her foot. Laughing like a small child, she chased it and tried to catch it in her cupped hand. When they came to a fruit orchard, Mia picked a guava leaf and crushed it in her hand to enjoy its wondrous fragrance. She did the same with a lemon leaf, and felt her whole being refreshed.

After passing a grove of green bamboo, they reached the outskirts of the highland village. Two young girls drawing water at the well stared at Mia's strange clothes. Feeling self-conscious, Mia walked by quickly. Beyond the well, a woman vendor was selling red beans with rice dumplings and coconut milk. Mia's eyes sparkled. Tao bought her two bowls of the sweet treat. It had been so long since Mia had tasted food so delicious, she easily ate both bowls.

Tao and Mia saw the village children flying a kite. Mia asked if they could follow the children, and she watched with delight as one boy lifted the kite and ran, while another held the string and chased after him. When they had picked up speed, the boy with the kite released it to the wind, and it flew higher and higher as he unwound more and more of the string.

As she watched the kite soar, Mia's thoughts turned to the moon. It was already late afternoon, and Dan and the children would be home soon. Mia said to Tao, "I must return now. Please take me back to the bamboo tree." Tao did not answer. Guessing that he wanted to persuade her to remain on earth for a few more days, Mia said, "I can't possibly stay any longer, Tao. Dan and the children will be waiting for me. I'll come back to visit again when I have a chance."

Tao remained silent. His expression was a strange mixture of regret and fear. Despite Mia's pleas, he did not move from where he sat. Exasperated, Mia stood up and said, "Very well, if you won't take me back to the tree, I'll go by myself." Hastily, she walked back in the direction of her abandoned hut, and Tao ran after her. Mia slowed her pace to allow him to catch up, and then quickened her steps again. They reached her old hut just as darkness was beginning to settle on the forest. The moon had risen. Mia put her arms around the tree and said farewell to Tao.

She had just begun to climb when Tao finally spoke, "Mia, it is no longer possible for you to return to the moon." Before she could question him, Mia noticed the sections of bamboo trunk strewn about the forest floor. Looking up, she discovered with a shock that the tree rose no more than twenty or thirty feet. "Tao, what happened? The tree has been chopped down!" she exclaimed.

Mia grew even more frightened when she saw Tao cover his face with his hands without answering her. She grabbed his shoulders and cried, "Did you chop down the tree, Tao? Answer me! Did you chop it down?"

Mia began to sob so violently that her eyes turned red and her hair fell in tangles across her face. She beat her hands against her chest, and then pounded Tao's shoulders. She screamed in his ear, "Tell me! Are you deaf? Why did you chop it down?"

"Because I love you too much," was Tao's only reply. He again covered his face with his hands in an expression of terrible remorse.

"Love me? You say you love me and yet you destroyed the only way I have to return to my husband and children? Tao! How could you have done this to me?"

The whole forest trembled with Mia's sobs. The moon shone so brilliantly that when Mia looked up, she could not make out anything at all. Knowing that her husband and children were waiting for her made her tears fall like rain. Mia cried for seven days and nights. She did not eat or sleep. Silently, Tao cut bamboo branches to repair the roof of her old hut to protect her from the sun and rain. He brought fruit for her to eat and water for her to drink, but she would have none of it. When her throat grew unbearably parched, she ran alone to the spring and scooped up a handful of water to drink. She rinsed her face and sat quietly by the spring for a long time. But thoughts of her husband and children soon brought back her tears. She was beyond comfort.

Tao made Mia some rice porridge, but when he offered it, she pushed his hand away. He placed the bowl beside her sleeping mat, but two days passed and Mia still had not touched the porridge. He made a fresh bowl and offered it to her, and again she pushed his hand away. But this time he did not put the bowl down. He continued to hold it before her. When his right hand grew weary, he switched the bowl to his left. He spent the entire night sitting before her, switching the bowl back and forth in his hands. At daybreak, unable to stand it any longer, Mia grabbed the bowl and placed it by her sleeping mat. But she did not eat any of the porridge.

Tao spent the day in the forest chopping wood to build furniture for the hut. When he returned in the evening, he was overjoyed to see an empty bowl beside Mia's mat. The fruit he had placed in the same spot was also gone. At last Mia had eaten. Tao gently placed his hand on her shoulder, but she pushed it away.

Tao was not disheartened, for he knew that Mia had wept all her tears and he must only be patient. Quietly, he repaired the thatched roof and transformed the hut into a comfortable home. One day he took courage again and placed his hand on Mia's shoulder. This time Mia did not push his hand away. She had forgiven him, and she had become resigned to her circumstances.

Tao cleared a section of forest and planted rice and corn. Together he and Mia started a new life. Sometimes they went to the highland market to sell firewood in order to buy sugar and salt, but Mia never returned to her own village for fear of meeting her aunt. Whenever she thought of her husband and children alone on the moon, she covered her face and wept. On full moon nights, she sat alone and gazed at the moon. But no matter how hard she looked, she never saw Dan, Summer, or Spring.

At the year's end, Tao suggested they pack their possessions and move to the highland village. He hoped that village life with its bustling market and friendly neighbors might help Mia think less often of her old family. They moved and Tao wasted no time planting rice fields and fruit orchards. Mia took up the craft of weaving.

In the autumn of the following year, on the full moon of the eighth month, Mia gave birth to a lovely baby girl. They named her Autumn. With little Autumn to care for, Mia's spirits brightened. It was as though her heart put forth new roots which went deep into the heart of the earth. This renewed connection to her homeland made Mia's eyes and hair shine again. One day Mia sang this lullaby to Autumn:

> Making soup with young bamboo shoots and
>   small fishes of the mountain spring,
> From now on, Mother must change sadness to
>   joy, O my beloved child.

Mia's garden was fragrant with the mint and coriander she had planted. The vines which climbed the trellis were heavy with melons and squash.

✿ ✿ ✿

With Spring in his right arm and Summer in his left, Dan entered the house and cheerfully called out, "We're home!" But the house was strangely cold and empty. Startled, Dan put the children down and went outside to look for Mia. She was nowhere

in sight. Ghostly shadows flitted across the empty
wheat fields. Dan walked to the melon field and
found Mia's footprints along with some the size of
a man's. Anxiously, Dan ran towards the bamboo
tree. It was no longer there. Though he peered far
below, there was no sign of fluttering leaves. He
knew the tree had been chopped down.

Dan returned to the house. He gathered his
children in his arms and wept. The house was
dark. No one had lit the lamps or cooked a meal.
His house was as cold as a coffin. Spring and
Summer both called out, "Mama!" Dan went to the
kitchen to find some leftovers for his children to
eat.

Days passed and Mia did not return. Dan did
his best to care for the children and to keep on living as before, but it was difficult. He thought it
would have been better if Mia had never come to
the moon, than to come and then abandon them.
He felt as though Mia had taken the meaning of
life with her. Though he often looked down to
earth while hoeing his fields, he never saw Mia.
"Why did you leave us, Mia?" was his constant
thought.

That year, the moon suffered a terrible drought.
Without rain, Dan's harvest was a failure. The
children still cried constantly for their mother.
Dan cried, too, when he tried to console them. One
day when he returned from working in the fields,
he could not find either of the children. Dan
looked everywhere, until finally he knelt down by
the spot where they often sat huddled together, crying for their mother, and there he found a large
puddle of water. Dan understood that his children

had cried until they turned into a puddle of tears. He touched the water with his finger and placed it on his tongue. The salty taste told him that these were truly his children's tears. Unable to contain his pain, he began to weep until he, too, was transformed into a stream of tears that joined the tears of his children.

The heat of the sun caused the large puddle of tears to evaporate and form a small gathering of clouds which traveled on the wind and wandered back and forth over the earth's surface, as if searching for something. The clouds wandered until one day they came to pause over Mia's backyard.

It was an oppressively hot, humid day. Tao and Autumn had gone to the market. Mia had waited all day in vain for the clouds to burst into rain and offer some relief. She decided to draw cool water from the well behind the house in order to take a shower. Around the well Mia had planted a dark green hedge of hibiscus dotted with flowers the color of bright flames. She undressed and splashed herself with buckets of cool water. She was startled by the rumble of nearby thunder. She looked up and saw a formation of clouds hovering above her. Of course, Mia did not know that these clouds were her husband and children from the moon. Still, she could not help staring at them.

The clouds recognized Mia and instantly burst into streams of rain that cascaded over her. The raindrops were warm and comforting on Mia's skin. As the water touched her skin, it began to assume shapes. In an instant, Dan and the two children materialized before Mia's eyes. Mia was ecstatic. She embraced Summer and Spring and then turned to Dan, her heart overflowing with happiness. She did not need to know how they made it to earth. They were beside her!

Mia got dressed and led Dan and the children into the house. Dan spoke first, "Why did you leave us, Mia! Didn't you love us anymore?"

Her eyes clouded with tears as she answered, "Of course, I loved you. I was homesick for the earth and intended to visit for only a few hours. But the bamboo tree was chopped down. I cried without stopping for many days. All these years I have longed for you and the children. I never meant to abandon you."

Mia recounted every detail of what had happened. When she finished speaking, Dan said, "Well, now that we have found you, we can return to the moon together." He did not know how they would do so, but with Mia back, he was sure they could find a way.

Mia hesitated. On the moon she would have Dan, Spring and Summer. But she would lose Autumn and Tao. Nearly three years of life with Tao had bonded her to him. If she returned to the moon, she would surely miss him and she knew she would long terribly for Autumn. "On earth I miss the moon. I long for Dan, Spring, and Summer. On the moon I would long for Tao and Autumn. What should I do?"

At just that moment, Mia heard Autumn's laughter coming from the front gate. Tao had returned from the market. Panic-stricken, Mia gasped in terror. Not knowing which family to choose, she grabbed a knife from a corner of the room and plunged it into her head.

It was the exact moment of noon, and the sun was poised directly above them. Unknown to them all, Mia had plunged the knife into her head at a most sacred and magical moment, and something wondrous occurred. The knife, as if it had a will of its own, proceeded to cleanly cut through Mia's head, neck and body, dividing Mia into two identical and whole Mias. The only thing distinguishing them from the original Mia was their smaller size. One Mia, whose hand still held the knife, said to the other Mia, "Sister, you take Dan and find a way to return to the moon. I'll stay here."

Moon Mia picked up her two children and walked with Dan out the back door. Everything happened so quickly that Dan forgot to say farewell to the other Mia. They walked past the well and followed the path by the rice field.

Meanwhile, Tao and Autumn entered by the front door. "Anyone home? We're back from the market," called Tao. He saw Mia sitting by the loom, busily weaving. She did not return his greeting. He gazed at her strangely and then lifted her to her feet. He looked into her eyes and uttered, "How strange indeed, Mia! I recognize your face and body, but why are you so small today?' Mia replied, "Because this is only half of me. The other half has returned with Dan to the moon."

❊   ❊   ❊

Moon Mia led Dan and the two children beyond Tao's fields to the outskirts of the village in order to avoid being seen by anyone. She did not know where to take them, when she suddenly remembered her old house in the forest which Tao had rebuilt. Since Tao and Mia had gone to live in the highland village, no one had tended either the house or the field. She led Dan and the children to her old home in the forest.

Much had fallen into disrepair, but together Dan and Mia fixed up the house and recultivated the fields. In time, they sowed rice, corn, and other vegetables, and raised some chickens. Summer and Spring wandered freely among the forest hills, and their mother taught them which fruits were good to eat.

Mia showed Dan the stream where long ago he had smiled at her. They sat on a large rock by the stream and watched the moon rise. Mia asked Dan what had happened on the moon since the day she had returned to earth. He told her everything, careful not to leave out any detail. He told her how they had cried so hard that they had turned into a great puddle of tears. He mused, "Perhaps the ocean itself is salty from the tears people have shed. Throughout the ages, who can say how many wives have been separated from their husbands, children torn from their parents, brothers and sisters forced to part—none of them knowing if they would ever see each other again. Now we are together and I will never allow us to be separated."

Tears fell from Mia's eyes as she and Dan sat bathed by the light of the moon. They both gazed at the moon. After a long moment, Mia noticed that tears glistened on Dan's eyelashes. She knew he missed the moon, just as she had once missed the earth. She remembered how she felt when she had first returned, how smelling the guava and lemon leaves had filled her heart with an immense love for her homeland. She remembered how precious it had been to hear a buffalo boy's song, watch children fly a kite, gather tamarind fruit, and taste familiar foods again. Now it was the same for Dan. He missed his life on the moon—its homes, fields, foods, bird songs, plants, and the way people conversed with each other.

Mia felt greater love for Dan than she ever had before. She placed her hand on his shoulder and said, "I know how much you miss home. Everything is strange to you—the food, the animals, the language—but you have me and the children. Now you know that we will never be apart." Mia paused for a moment, and then continued, "You and the children were not able to live without me, but now we are together. Be patient and find happiness here. Who knows? Some day we may find a way to return to the moon."

Dan looked at her and asked, "If we are able to return to the moon, will you still long for the earth? Will you leave us as you did before?" Mia took Dan's hand and answered with all her heart, "No, never. I have lived on the earth, and I have lived on the moon. Half of me will always remain on the earth, and half of me will be free to live on the moon. You know, when I returned to earth, I missed my life on the moon. I was homesick, not just for you and the children, but also for the trees and grasses, the birds and streams, and the foods you taught me to cook."

Dan was filled with happiness to hear Mia speak her heart's truth. Together they stood and walked back to the house. They covered the children, who were already asleep, with a light mat, and then lay down to sleep themselves.

❀ ❀ ❀

Earth Mia lived happily with Tao and Autumn. Though she was Earth Mia, she was no different from Moon Mia. She was neither younger nor smaller. Her heart filled with warm affection, and she smiled whenever she thought of Moon Mia. She was at ease, knowing that her identical half was caring for Dan and the children. She knew they would have happiness with Moon Mia by their side. Whatever she could do, Moon Mia could do as well. She even believed that Moon Mia had returned to the moon with Dan, Summer, and Spring, though how, she could not guess. She smiled whenever she thought of her old house on the moon with its many windows and solid walls, and the fields of curious rice and melons. It was true, the moon did not resemble the earth at all.

Earth Mia regained her original size in just three days, thanks to a sudden increase in appetite. She thought of herself as a plant from which a cutting had been made to start a new plant. The new plant continued the life of the original plant in putting forth buds, leaves, flowers, and fruit—two plants but also one. One plant became two, and could have just as easily become five or ten new plants.

Mia found herself smiling, as she remembered her mother who had been so beautiful. Once she happened upon her mother massaging her grandmother's head with balm to ease a headache. Mia remembered grabbing hold of her mother's sleeve to play. Suddenly, a hissing sound of boiling water came from the kitchen. Mia's mother cried, "Oh dear, the soup is boiling over!" She put down the massage balm, removed Mia's hand from her sleeve, and started to run to the kitchen, just as her husband called, "Dear, come quick, I can't open the stable door without help!" Mia's mother stood between the kitchen and the front door, torn between reducing the fire on the stove and running to assist her husband. She turned to Mia and exclaimed, "If I only had four arms I could cook the soup, massage your grandmother's forehead, open the stable door with your father, and keep you from running out to the pond! But I only have two arms!"

Mia had thought, at the time, how strange a person with four arms would look. But a few days later, her mother took her to a temple where she saw a Buddha with many arms, each holding something different—a pen, a lotus flower, a flute—to perform a different task. Mia's mother told her it was Kwan Yin Bodhisattva who had a thousand arms to perform a thousand deeds, and a thousand eyes to see a thousand things. Mia's mother had only wished for four arms. Mia wondered if that was why her mother came to offer incense to Kwan Yin.

But in truth, Mia's mother did not really need four arms. With only two, she cared for Mia's grandmother, assisted her husband, cared for Mia, managed the household tasks, and worked in the garden. She was as talented as Kwan Yin. It was sad she had passed away early, leaving Mia to fall into the hands of her cruel aunt.

As Mia sat weaving cloth at her loom, her thoughts drifted back to the day Dan came to plead with her to return to the moon. She remembered that fateful moment when she heard Tao returning from the market while Dan stood before her. She remembered the terrible panic and anguish in her heart. If it had not been for a sacred moment in time, she would now be dead, leaving both families to suffer.

Mia knew other village women who expressed the desire to turn into four or five persons—one to care for their own parents, one to care for their husband's parents, one to care for their husband and children, another to cook the meals and tend the garden. Mia wished everyone could divide themselves as she had, like a plant that puts forth shoots to create new plants.

Dan transformed the forest hut into a spacious, comfortable home. The rice and corn plants in the fields grew green and healthy. Dan became accustomed to eating earth foods such as boiled corn, fish cake, manioc soup, and salted fish. When he told Mia that he found these dishes as delicious as his favorite moon foods, her face broke into a smile.

With Dan and the two children beside her, Mia felt as though she possessed the moon, and she no longer missed or longed for it. But she knew that, though Dan had found happiness on the earth, his happiness was incomplete. Unlike Mia, he still distinguished between the moon and the earth. She had told him that if she returned to the moon she would no longer miss the earth. She was able to say that because, for her, the earth was no longer the earth and the moon was no longer the moon. Both earth and moon lived in her own heart, and Mia was at peace. She hoped to share that peace with her husband and children. But she knew that Spring, Summer, and their father, having been born on the moon, missed their old life.

One day while returning with water from the well, Mia heard Spring calling, "Mother, Mother! Come and see this strange plant!"

Mia put down her carrying pole and asked, "Where, my daughter?"

Spring tugged at her sleeve and led her to the edge of the garden. "It's so strange, Mother. I saw a new little bamboo shoot, as rosy as a jewel and fragrant as an orange blossom!"

"Where was it, child?"

While Spring pointed to the place, Mia realized she was looking at the roots of the old bamboo tree. The trunk of the old tree had long since died, and Mia never imagined a new shoot would sprout by its side. She told Spring to run and find Dan. When he arrived from the fields carrying a pole heavily laden with pumpkins, Mia showed him the bamboo shoot.

"Look, Dan, this old tree is the very one that once rose to the moon, the one on which I climbed to the moon, the one which was later chopped down. It has given forth a new little sprout. This sprout will become a mighty tree just like its parent. We shall be able to return to the moon!"

Dan understood. His shining eyes warmed Mia's heart. When Summer and Spring heard they would be able to return to the moon, they clapped their hands with joy. Mia had never seen her husband and children so happy.

"Summer," she said, "give me a watering can. Dan, bring me a bucket of water. We must water this bamboo shoot so it can quickly grow into a tree."

From that moment on, not a day passed that they did not carefully tend their bamboo tree, their source of hope.

Peony Blossoms

Peony Blossoms

Tanh rang the bell and waited for his nephew, Thi, to come to the gate and greet him. Thi was a pale, delicate eight-year-old, whose large black eyes revealed how very much he loved his uncle. Each Saturday he would firmly take hold of Uncle Tanh's hand and lead him into the garden, where they would spend more than half an hour wandering among the cool shade trees. Thi would ask questions on every subject imaginable.

Thi's family lived in an elegant house surrounded by six acres of land. They were fortunate, as it was difficult to find such a lovely place so close to Montpellier, an industrial city in the south of France. Doan, Thi's father, worked for the Institute of Physics Research and taught at the University of Montpellier.

But on that Saturday it was Tuyet, Thi's mother, who met Tanh at the gate. "Your little nephew has been sick in bed since yesterday," Tuyet told him, with a touch of worry in her voice.

Sister and brother followed the white gravel walkway towards the house. They went into Thi's room, and saw that the boy's eyes were closed. "He must be asleep," Tuyet said. "Otherwise he would have opened his eyes and smiled at his dear Uncle." She placed her hand gently on his forehead, lifted the cotton blanket over his chest, and turned to Tanh, "Yes, he's finally dozed off. Let's sit in the living room."

Tuyet told her brother about Thi's illness. The day before, Thi had complained of a headache. Tuyet gave him a sugar-coated aspirin and coaxed him into drinking a glass of milk. At lunch time, the boy did not eat at all, and he began to run a fever, so Tuyet phoned Dr. Peltier. At three in the afternoon, the doctor came and diagnosed the symptoms as nothing more than a common cold. He left Thi another bottle of sugar-coated pills. At six, Thi seemed better, and he ate a few spoonfuls of soup. But by nine o'clock, his forehead was hot as an ember. Thi's parents took his temperature: it was 104 degrees Fahrenheit. In a panic, Tuyet phoned Dr. Peltier, who came and again reassured Tuyet that it was not particularly serious. "Let him sleep through the night," he said, "and tomorrow he will be fine." The doctor promised to return the next day. That night, Thi did not sleep at all, and his mother could not sleep either. She wanted to phone the doctor but, reluctant to impose again, she decided to wait. "He will be back tomorrow," she consoled herself. But it was not until moments before Tanh arrived that the boy finally fell asleep.

Tanh listened attentively, and told his sister, "I am sure our dear Thi will be fine. It is probably a flu or something. Let's not worry." And he asked her if she had any news from friends and family back home in Vietnam.

Half an hour later they were still talking when the boy's father, Doan, emerged from his study. He walked past his wife directly to Tanh, and, holding his brother-in-law's arm, he said, "I hope you will stay for lunch. I have a meeting at the university this afternoon, and your sister is so worried about her little rascal, I'd be more comfortable if you stayed with her." Tanh agreed, and Doan quickly prepared to go.

Tuyet said, "I'm so glad you'll be staying. Let me see what we've got for lunch."

"Take your time, there's no hurry," her brother replied. "I'll be out in the garden."

Doan's garden was large and well-tended. It was early May, and the leaves were young and green. The linden trees, in particular, were bursting with new growth. "In a couple of weeks," Tanh thought, "I can come and pick the blossoms for tea." Tanh loved linden tea. It refreshed him and helped him relax after long hours at work on his paintings. He thought, "How funny. The Chinese call lindens *bodhi* trees, and their blossoms, *bodhi* flowers, flowers of awakening." Then he walked to the wooden bench below the large chestnut tree. The straight branches, loaded with blossoms, reminded Tanh of the candlesticks in Buddhist temples.

Tanh knew that if Thi were present, the boy would be asking dozens of questions, including many Tanh would not be able to answer. One time, Thi pointed to a spot on the chestnut tree and asked what color it was. It was a patch of moss somewhere between green and purple, certainly not any kind of blue. Tanh did not know what to call it, so he answered, "It's just that color!" The boy understood, and was satisfied.

Tanh felt very close to Thi. He had often used that color, himself, in his paintings. In fact, Tanh was so familiar with it that he never felt the need to name it. Similarly, names were not important in the manner of greeting people in Vietnam. If you met someone and smiled, or held their hand, that was enough. It was more important to remember the person than his name or position.

Tanh remembered with delight another incident that made him feel close to his nephew. Tuyet had given Thi a peach and, rather than eat it, Thi studied it and held it against his cheek. Tuyet told him, "Uncle Tanh brought us plenty of peaches, so you eat this one and have another one later." Thi shook his head to say he did not want another peach.

When Tanh later reminded him of the exchange, Thi told him, "When I looked at that peach, I realized it was a miraculous creation. How many months it must have taken for its mother, the tree, to create it! How many brothers and sisters it must have! I held it against my cheek and enjoyed its friendship." Thi had treated the peach as a being worthy of his full attention, not just as something to ingest. When he ended up biting into the fruit and swallowing it, his uncle had teased, "There goes your 'friend'!" Thi had laughed too when he saw his uncle laughing.

The warmth expressed between uncle and nephew was not often the case between father and son. Doan was immersed in his teaching and research, and rarely had time for even a walk in the garden with Thi. He was certainly a kind, considerate man, but physics was his passion, and he was always absorbed in it. Doan, preoccupied with mathematical determinants, was worlds away from his son's broad face and bright eyes. He could use mathematics to describe the physical laws which control the reflection and travel of light, but he could not see the simple yearnings of his little boy.

Now Thi was ill, and Tanh sat alone beneath the chestnut tree. He thought about the gap between Doan's world of elementary particles and Thi's world of feelings and sensations. Tanh understood Doan's love of physics and math. As an artist, he knew that both science and art can engage one so completely that one overlooks the details of everyday life. Although he could not converse with his brother-in-law in technical language, Tanh understood that the world of elementary particles could be more real to Doan than the world of the senses was for his nephew and himself.

Once, while they were having coffee together, Tanh chided Doan, "You know, it's possible that your subatomic world is only a world of ghosts."

Doan laughed. "Yes, sometimes I think so too. But those ghosts are real, and that is why I spend so much time looking for them. You know, atoms and electrons do not occupy specific locations in space and time. As we approach them, they flee. What we think of as solid or permanent simply does not exist in the subatomic world."

"Then it must be easier to demonstrate interconnectedness and impermanence in that world than in everyday life."

Doan nodded. "Yes, of course. Look for yourself. In the world of our senses, a cup of coffee is a cup of coffee. It cannot be both a cup of coffee and a glass of wine. Tanh is Tanh. You cannot be at the same time Tanh and Doan. But in the world of elementary particles, electrons can appear as either particles or waves. Are they two things at the same time? This gives scientists headaches!"

"I see. So you scientists have given up?"

"No. We recognize them as both one thing and two things, and we call them 'wavicles,' which means both wave and particle. We know that we cannot adopt the images of ordinary life to describe the entities of the subatomic world. After all, how can we call an electron solid or permanent when it is only movement? How can we follow it on even one trajectory? We cannot 'recognize' an electron because we cannot grasp its 'identity.' We can see the difference between Tanh and Doan— each of us can have a separate I.D. card—but we cannot distinguish between two electrons."

As Doan explained how elementary particles do not have separate "selves," Tanh remembered reading that they do not even act according to the rules of cause and effect or the laws of statistics. He sympathized with scientists working to rid themselves of the most common assumptions about life. Ultimately, they would even have to go beyond even the scientific method itself! With what mind could they then enter the world of elementary particles?

Tanh always enjoyed his conversations with Doan, as he found his brother-in-law to be remarkably broad-minded and intelligent. They often stayed up until three in the morning discussing science, art, and even Buddhist philosophy.

Tuyet came out to the garden and found her brother sitting under the chestnut tree. "Thi is awake and wants to see you," she said. "He looks much better. Can you sit with him while I finish preparing lunch? And please do stay for dinner as well."

"I'd be happy to," he said, as they walked back to the house together.

As soon as his uncle appeared, Thi stretched out his arms to embrace him. "Because you are sick, I had to go to the garden all by myself," Tanh said, lifting the boy above him.

Thi's eyes brightened as he thought about the garden. "Next week, I'll walk with you. The shiny, green peony buds have blossomed into beautiful flowers. Did you see them?"

"No, I didn't. I only walked as far as the chestnut tree. I'll wait until next week and we can see them together. Did you know that peonies are *mau-don* in Vietnamese?"

Thi's French was much better than his Vietnamese. Sometimes, Tanh spoke to him in French with the sort of intimacy children enjoy, but he made it a point to keep him from forgetting his Vietnamese. Tanh was patient, and Tuyet was always happy to see her brother and her son speaking together in her native tongue. His uncle always had the impression that when Thi spoke French, he was not the same child as when he spoke Vietnamese. It was as if he had two souls, one for each language. Tanh smiled to himself, for he remembered the conversation with Doan about the two different natures of an electron.

After a short conversation, Tanh left Thi's bedroom and went to the kitchen. Tuyet asked her brother about his art. "I haven't painted for months. Some big change is going on in me. I have been watching it closely, and I don't want to interfere with it."

Tuyet often worried about her brother's ability to support himself. She knew that he was an artist with integrity, who did not spend time developing styles to please wealthy patrons. Tanh believed that an artist needed only a few lines, shapes, and colors to make a painting, just as a writer needs only a few words to create a good poem. Once Tanh knew clearly what he wanted to express in his art, it came forth easily.

But there were times when he would not even touch his brushes, for he knew that the seed within him was not yet ripe. The true work of an artist, Tanh believed, always began with awareness of his deepest inner turmoil. He needed to continuously observe it with great care and acceptance. Only after such feelings completed their cycle and became transformed could they express themselves in a painting. At such times, an artist needed only to hold his brush, and the form and style would manifest. Mixing colors and handling brushes were secondary to the vital technique of stopping, observing, and entering life itself. For Tanh, the practice of art lay in nurturing his inner life and being attentive to small changes, not in acquiring technical or stylistic originality.

Tanh never regarded fallow periods as a waste of time. If he did not have paintings for sale, he was content to work as a housepainter. He told Tuyet many times, "Don't worry. Before I go broke, I will ask you for a little rice."

Tuyet would always tell him, "Heavens. I would like nothing better than for you to eat with us ev-

ery day! Thi especially would love it. In fact, why
don't you move in with us? We have plenty of
room. We could turn the basement into a studio.
Why must you pay rent when you could be so comfortable here?"

Tanh looked at his sister and smiled. "It's really quite pleasant at home. I'm used to it, my rent
is reasonable, and I enjoy traveling between our
two places."

"You are so stubborn, my dear brother! But I
won't insist. I think you like your privacy too
much. Now let me serve our lunch."

❊ ❊ ❊

Tanh woke suddenly at two in the morning. He had
had a strange dream, and his forehead was wet
with perspiration. He reached for a wash cloth and
wiped the moisture. Then he lay on his back, his
arms and legs outstretched, and began a slow, deep
breathing exercise to help regain calmness in body
and mind.

In the dream, Tanh had been holding little
Thi's hand, and they were wandering together in a
forest filled with beautiful trees and wildflowers.
They were breaking small twigs and gathering
leaves to build a small "palace," when suddenly the
sky darkened and they could not even see each
other's faces.

Tanh called out for Thi, but there was no reply.
He reached out, groping in the darkness. Even the
trees and bushes seemed to have disappeared. He

reached for the ground, but it had become a kind of liquid, and he lost his balance and fell. Struggling in what seemed like water, he felt something and grasped it. It was Thi's arm. The two of them managed to float and tread water for a long time. Finally they reached a tree and climbed up onto it. By then, it was daylight, and they saw that the forest had disappeared.

Tanh took Thi's hand, and they ran across vast, empty stretches of land bristling with sharp rocks, glass shards, and clumps of burned-out, blackened trees. Overhead, a storm was approaching and Tanh could hear a screaming crowd angrily pursuing them. He looked for a safe shelter but there was only emptiness and destruction around them. Tanh and Thi realized it was useless to run any further, and they stood still, ready to face their pursuers. The screams stopped, and the gathering storm froze in stillness.

At this point, Tanh awoke. He knew he had to continue concentrating on his gentle, deep breathing, in order to invite a thought that could help him understand the dream. He did not want to use reason to arrive at an explanation, for he felt that his intuition could offer him a much deeper understanding. A long while passed, and no insight arose, but Tanh did feel refreshed from the breathing exercise. He stood up, walked slowly to the bathroom, and turned on the shower. The fine jets of warm water soothed him. After a few minutes, he turned off the water, dried himself carefully, and put on some comfortable clothes.

In his study, Tanh lit a stick of fragrant incense and sat down cross-legged on a folded blan-

ket on the floor. Sitting meditation was an important part of his work. As always, he focused his
mind on his breathing. About twenty minutes
later, he let go of conscious deep breathing and allowed his mind to go wherever it wanted, continuing to watch it, much as a buffalo boy watches
his herd roaming freely in a grassy field.

Tanh began to see images of himself in the village along the river bank where he had grown up. It
was a small village crossed by the Hau Giang River
in the province of Long Xuyen. Rich, immense rice
fields flourished along both sides of the river. As a
child, Tanh had run barefoot with his friends on
the dikes of those rice fields, digging for earth-
worms, catching fish, setting shrimp traps, and
hunting for black crickets. What had become of
those friends? Some had died on battlefields, others were in "re-education" camps, and others, he
had learned, had simply vanished without a trace.
He knew that Que, his closest friend in grade
school, had been killed in the Battle of Pleime.
"His body must be one with the earth by now,"
Tanh thought. Many boys of the younger genera-
tion had been killed by bullets and bombs. His own
nephew Thi was more fortunate. Although both his
parents were Vietnamese, he was born in France.
His collective karma was linked with other Vietnamese children, but his personal karma set him
apart, providing him with advantages that children in Vietnam couldn't even imagine.

Ever since Tanh had arrived in France, whenever he saw children playing in a schoolyard or on
a sidewalk, his thoughts always went back to the
children of Vietnam. Tanh had held in his arms

many little bodies torn apart by bullets or bomb shrapnel, and many times he had had to bury them with his own hands. As a member of the ambulance team of the Buddhist Youth Association, Tanh had braved many dangers to help wounded, helpless civilians.

Tanh could never forget holding the limp body of a four-year-old girl, her head twisted to one side, her hair matted with blood. He didn't have time to shed even a single tear for her, as hundreds of others were in great need, crying out for help from him and his comrades. He only had two or three seconds to look at that young girl, but they were seconds he could never forget. Tanh felt torn apart inside. The more pain and suffering he saw, the deeper the roots of his being went down into the soil of his homeland.

It was now four years since he boarded the plane which took him to Paris for the "Family Reuniting Program." How could he have left Vietnam? Not for his own future. Not for his art. Certainly not for a comfortable existence. Was it for freedom? Would personal freedom for someone whose life had such deep links with the soil of his homeland be possible? Tanh shook his head in doubt. He did not want to think any further.

His friend Que—even his bones must have disintegrated by now. And Truc, his elder brother, had been a communications officer in the South Vietnamese Army when he was lost in action in 1972, and his remains still had not been found. Truc's bones, too, must have become soil somewhere in the mountains along the Laotian border. And the little girl who had died in his arms, had her little bones gone back to the earth of her people? Tanh could still recall the precise location of her small grave within the burial compound of the Congregation of Binh Dinh Province. Had her flesh become soil yet? He had buried her with neither casket nor ritual. He did not know her name, or her family. All he could do, pushing earth back into the hole in the ground, was to say the name of Amidha Buddha over and over again.

Tanh's parents were killed when a bomb destroyed their home in Long Xuyen. He was nineteen at the time. Several years later, he went back to his village and sat on the mound of bricks, tiles, plaster, and wood where his ancestral house had stood. Sitting there, he caught sight of one tiny wildflower with five purple petals growing through a crack in the stone, and its fragile beauty touched him deeply. He realized that the flower did not mind the destruction at all. Here was life in all its power and wonder springing forth in the midst of chaos, hatred, and death.

The delicate flower called out to Tanh and told him that although the reality of life is suffering, suffering is not enough. Nothing exists forever; everything is interconnected. Life is the ceaseless movement of creation and destruction. Tanh realized that joy and pain, far from being in conflict with one another, are complementary in the same way as creation and destruction.

The wildflower helped Tanh understand the teachings of Toan, the elderly sculptor under whom he studied at the Art Institute. Toan, when holding a chisel and a mallet, or manipulating clay, looked like an ancient priest performing a sacred ritual.

He was at once gentle and powerful, graceful yet solemn. He did not produce much, but whatever art he did create was rich and vigorous.

Once he took Tanh to the An Quang Pagoda to show him his sculpture of Manjushri, the Bodhisattva of Great Understanding. After that, Tanh frequently returned to An Quang to see his teacher's work. Looking at the statue, Tanh knew that no artist could have carved such a beautiful figure without having suffered and loved to such a great extent.

Here was the face of a being who had a deep knowledge of all existence. Facing the wooden Bodhisattva's carved eyes, one could not avoid noticing the true nature of all joy and pain. Viewers were opened by Manjushri's gaze, just as flowers open their petals to the sun for illumination. His eyes looked at the beholder, not with a look that probed or judged, but with one that understood and calmed.

It was the look of compassion, confirmed by the smile on Manjushri's face. Only one who had known the deepest pain could smile so gently, and look on the world with such compassionate eyes. The Bodhisattva's posture and the position of his hands were those of a sympathetic human being, not of a supernatural god. Toan's figure communicated that a human being, once he or she becomes deeply human, can become a Buddha. The Bodhisattva sat perfectly still, fearless and complete, but not at all remote.

Tanh had visited Toan often, and had begun to learn to sit in meditation. "Sitting," Toan told him, "is a way to help artistic inspiration ripen before it transforms into a work of art." Toan also helped Tanh understand the relationship between his homeland, Vietnam, and himself, an artist: "Every nation and its people go through times of glory, as well as times of suffering. An artist, by expressing his own hopes and pains, can speak for a nation, because the artist's sentiments are so deeply resonant with those of his people." Tanh had not fully understood Toan's words until he saw the wildflower springing up amidst the rubble of the war.

Often Tanh looked at his nephew Thi and thought, "Here is a child born and raised in a country without war, a child well loved and cared for by his parents and other adults around him, and provided for with many material comforts." Then he thought of the children whose bodies were mangled by bombs and bullets, and children who wandered about cold and hungry, lost in a world of hatred.

He recalled the dream that had awakened him during the night. He was holding Thi's hand, and they were running, while a storm was about to break. Tanh realized that his running expressed his desire to escape death, despair, and impermanence. He recalled the end of the dream. Knowing that it was impossible to hide, he had stopped running, and the screaming of the pursuing crowd ceased. Could the real enemy be his fear and pain, his yearning for an existence independent of the difficult conditions of this world? "Life brings us into the world and she buries us," Tanh thought. "There is no life without death, and no death without life. To accept life wholeheartedly is to accept both sides of life's reality." Tanh saw the little girl who had died in his arms, and she was smiling at him. What a miraculous smile! He saw that it was the same smile as Thi's. Yes, it was Thi smiling! The little girl experiencing the most horrible suffering and Thi with all his comforts, were the same child.

Though the war had ended five years before, and both uncle and nephew were living safely in a land of peace and democracy, the reality of Vietnam was alive within every cell of Tanh's body. The dream was not an illusion. It was as real as any physical object around him. He had climbed the steps and boarded the plane for France, but he had never left his homeland. He himself was his homeland.

Gently, Tanh came out of his meditation. He stood up and began walking slowly, making each step with the utmost care, as if he wanted to imprint his footprints clearly on the floor, on the earth itself. That morning, Tanh began a painting of little Thi standing next to a bouquet of peonies in full bloom. He worked all day and late into the night, only stopping for a piece of bread, an orange, and a glass of water. He then slept for four hours.

Early the next morning, after half-an-hour of meditation, he turned on his studio light and continued working. Several times before noon the doorbell rang, but he did not answer it. He did not want to see or talk to anyone while he was painting Thi.

He worked until midday Thursday. The painting, he thought, was completed. Perhaps a touch here, a slight change there, but that was all that was needed. Tanh plugged in the spotlight on the south wall, focused the light on his painting, and sat down to look at his work. Thi's smile was clear and bright like the peony blossom he held in his hand. It was the same smile as that of the little girl Tanh had seen during his meditative sitting. He painted his nephew wearing traditional Vietnamese gray pants and shirt, which the little girl who had died in his arms years ago also wore. "She has come back," Tanh thought. "She now lives in Thi and in all the children who are alive and walking the ground of his homeland."

O, children, as you walk towards the future, take with you the thousands of small ones who were struck down. We adults who have been blinded by ambition and hatred must step aside and let you pass. Little Thi will never die. In him, the past is alive, and through him, all children, dead and alive, can go forth and realize the future.

Tanh turned off the lights, closed the door to his studio, and walked up the staircase leading to the ground floor. He felt at peace. He wanted to eat lunch and take a short nap before putting the final touches on his painting, but when he passed his mailbox, he noticed an urgent message. It was from his sister: "I need you. Come right away. Tuyet." Tanh immediately changed into street clothes and headed for the bus stop.

❊ ❊ ❊

By Wednesday, Thi's fever had climbed to 105 degrees and he began vomiting. His head hurt terribly, and he could not stop screaming as he desperately pressed his hands against his temples. Thi's cries wrenched his parents' hearts. Tuyet frantically tried to comfort Thi, and Doan called Dr. Peltier. The doctor told them to bring the boy to the Children's Hospital immediately and he would meet them there. By the time they reached the hospital, Thi was barely conscious.

Thi was put through a variety of tests, and the doctors found that he had a tumor on his brain, and that he was also suffering from an attack of meningitis. His life was in immediate danger, and they decided to operate to remove the tumor.

It was fortunate that the finest resident surgeon at the Children's Hospital was present. Preparations took nearly three hours, and Thi was wheeled in and put face down on a specially equipped table.

Tuyet and Doan waited in a small room outside the operating room. Time seemed to stand still. Tuyet chanted under her breath, invoking the compassion of Kwan Yin Bodhisattva. But Doan could not pray. His heart was on fire. The more he thought about Dr. Peltier's misdiagnoses, the angrier he became. Three times the doctor had underestimated the seriousness of Thi's condition!

The operation was completed by nightfall, and Thi was still unconscious. Doan was told that the operation had gone smoothly but that the child's condition remained critical. Treatments with various serums, antibiotics, and cortisone were being carried out, and Thi was expected to regain consciousness in about six hours.

The hospital allowed only one person to remain with Thi, and Doan decided that it should be Tuyet. He told her to telephone immediately if there was any change; otherwise, she should just rest. As her husband was leaving, Tuyet asked him to pray very hard, and also to send a mailgram to her brother Tanh.

Doan could not eat any supper. He drank a glass of milk and sat waiting for his wife's call. He could not sit still, as if a fire burned under his chair. He got up and paced about from the sitting room to the kitchen, back to the sitting room, to the study, to Thi's room, then from Thi's room to his, and to Tuyet's bedroom. Everywhere he walked, he felt on fire. He returned to the sitting room, sat down in his familiar armchair for only a few minutes before he stood up again and continued walking. His old, comfortable chair was totally enveloped in fire.

By eleven o'clock at night, there was still no call from Tuyet, which meant that their son was still unconscious. Doan began to panic. He wanted to be calm, but there was nothing he could do. He knew that at that moment his wife was praying for their son, and he wished that he, too, had such a pure and simple faith. But he could not bring himself to believe that invoking Lord Buddha's name would in any way improve his son's chance of survival. Tuyet had often encouraged him to pray with her, but he never could. Until his son came out of mortal danger, he knew he would not be able to rest.

The clock on the wall struck midnight. Doan put on his pajamas and got into bed, hoping he would just drop off to sleep. But he could not even close his eyes. Then, only then, did he slowly and clearly begin to see the true face of his inner disquiet. The image of Thi kept appearing before him. He trembled as he thought of his son's mortality. He tossed and turned, trying to find a position which might be more restful, to no avail. His bed was on fire too. He felt as if he, Tuyet, Thi, and their entire house, were floating on the ocean and could be capsized by a wave at any moment. It was the first time he realized how entwined Thi's life was with his own. He saw that if Thi died, he would no longer be himself. He would also die. Thi was more than just his son. He was Doan himself.

For years, Doan thought that providing security and comfort for his son was all he needed to do. He was like a gardener who, after planting a healthy tree and giving it rich soil and a windbreak, leaves it to fend for itself. Suddenly he realized that Thi was not just a tree. He was also the gardener, and the heart of the gardener as well. If the tree died, so would the gardener.

Doan's family lived on solid ground, not in a boat tossed about on the sea. France was a country at peace. Montpellier was a city with all the opportunity in the world to bring forth the fruit of his son's learning and abilities. Thi was surrounded by love and care from his parents, his school, his society.

Doan knew about the dangers that refugees who escaped by sea had to face, including hunger, thirst, storms, and pirates. Just last month, he had read that fewer than fifty percent of all those who leave Vietnam by boat survive. He thought of the homeless and the destitute, the victims of the war, and he thought of himself. He was living in his own home, a charming house surrounded by trees and flowers, a house of love and tranquility. And yet, for a moment, he could see clearly that he, too, was bobbing up and down on the ocean. All his peace and security had evaporated, and his own fate was as uncertain as that of the boat people.

Doan's discovery was remarkable! Thi was not only his son, but Thi was Doan himself. Were Thi to die, Doan too would die. Even if Doan did not actually die, he would be only a shadow of himself. What a shocking insight! How could he ever fall asleep now that he knew this. He was like a man shot by an arrow. The shock, the pain, the reality of it all was so strong he could not even shut his eyes. Doan gave up trying to sleep. He went into the kitchen and made a cup of strong black coffee.

He knew that he had come face to face with a reality he had never faced before. His struggle for survival was as desperate as that of the refugees in their fragile boats. If he did not find a way to overcome his torments and worries, he too might drown. Tuyet had not telephoned and, he thought, if she did, it might be to tell him that Thi was still unconscious. All evening, Doan had been hoping for a call, and now he was afraid the phone might ring. But he had to stand firm, for the coming storm could bring them all down to the bottom of the sea. The night was only half over, and Doan imagined that his hair had turned white. He knew he had to fight. But with what weapons? Tuyet could pray, for she had her faith in the Buddha. Her brother Tanh knew how to sit quietly and meditate. Doan had neither Tuyet's faith nor Tanh's training. What about his scientific knowledge? How could it be of use to him in a time like this, a time when fear and uncertainty were so huge that he felt ready to burst into a thousand pieces?

It was now two-thirty in the morning. Doan had restlessly paced from room to room, rolled over in bed, and sat down and stood up hundreds of times. He had tried to read newspapers and books, and each time he could read only one or two lines. He asked himself who in the entire world would he most like to have next to him to share some of his anxiety and fear. He thought of his friends, and decided none of them would be able to do that. No one could come into his lonely world and be with him. He knew that it was easier to sit and face his torments by himself than to be with someone who could not share them with him. Then he thought of Tanh, and he realized that he would feel less lonely if Tanh were sitting with him now, even if silently. He knew that Tanh loved Thi as much as he and Tuyet loved the boy.

If only Tanh had a telephone, he would call him right away. However, he knew that Tanh was a free soul who might not even be at home tonight. He then remembered that he had not sent a mailgram to Tanh as Tuyet had asked him to do. He reached for the phone, dialed, and dictated the message on behalf of Tuyet, asking that her brother come over immediately. He set the phone down, turned on all the lights in the living room, and sat down again in his reclining chair. The phone message would not be delivered until eight o'clock, so the earliest that Tanh would arrive would be around ten. Doan knew that Tanh loved Thi very much and that news of the boy's condition would come as a great shock to him. But Doan could not imagine his brother-in-law reacting with the kind of panic he himself felt.

The clock on the wall rang three times. It was three in the morning. Doan knew that his son was still unconscious, and that his life was hanging by a thread. A frail, small body like Thi's, how could it survive both a brain tumor and meningitis? If Dr. Peltier were here, Doan would not spare his feelings.

Doan knew that Thi's condition pushed the limits of medical science. Only last January his friend Binh had died at the Lariboisière Hospital in Paris, even after successful brain surgery. "Faith in science is fine," Doan thought, "but in life one must also believe in miracles." He knew that his wife was praying now for such a miracle, invoking the names of the Compassionate and Healing Bodhisattvas. Doan desperately wished that he also could take refuge in such religious faith. But his interest in Buddhism was much more casual than the powerful faith of Tuyet or the practical and philosophical discipline of Tanh.

By now Doan was so tense that his brain felt as though it could explode. He stared at the telephone, wanting to call the hospital, but he knew it would be of no use. If and when Thi became conscious, Tuyet would rush to phone him. It was four in the morning. Doan lay on his bed with his arms and legs straight like a corpse. He got up, swallowed two aspirins with a glass of cool water, and went back to lie down, hoping the pills might calm his nerves. Half an hour later, his head was burning. He rubbed it with his hands for a while, then gave up. He went to the medicine chest and took out two capsules of Immenoctal, a powerful sleeping drug. After swallowing them, he turned off all the lights, even the tiny night-light in the bedroom, and went to bed again.

It was five-fifteen in the morning before he finally fell into a drugged sleep. He had frightening dreams, one after another. In the last one, he, Tuyet, and Thi were sitting in a small boat, being tossed in a rough sea. A wave as big as a mountain engulfed them. Doan screamed and woke up. He touched his forehead, which was drenched with sweat. His watch showed eight-twenty. He had slept for three hours, but he felt even more tired than before and his tenseness had not gone away. The more he tried to subdue his fears and worries, the more damage they seemed to inflict on his body.

The telephone rang. Doan's heart pounded in his chest. He ran to the living room. Yes, it was Tuyet. No, Thi was not yet conscious. Tuyet's voice was full of tears. Doan told her that he had sent a mailgram to Tanh, and that by ten he would be at their home. Tuyet said he should wait for Tanh, and the two of them could come to the hospital together. She promised him that she would call as soon as there was any news.

Setting the phone down, Doan realized that his son's condition was even more dangerous than he had feared. After speaking with his wife, his torment was even more devastating. When might they see any signs of improvement in Thi's condition? Tonight, tomorrow, the day after? Could he himself survive another day of this ordeal?

Doan sat motionless in his armchair. At this moment, his son was fighting for his life. Over and over, Doan muttered the same words to himself, "Keep it up, son, keep it up." Thi had to fight. And he, Doan, was fighting too. He did not have his wife's faith or his brother-in-law's meditation practice, and he could not borrow from them. What practice did he have that he could call his own? He thought about his vocation, his love of physics and mathematics. Was there anything in the research to which he had devoted years of his life that could help him now?

He asked himself that question, and suddenly he felt a strong urge to go to his study and sit at his desk. He went first to wash his face and put on a fresh shirt, and when he entered his study, Doan immediately felt rather relaxed. A pleasant feeling enveloped him as he again entered a world both physically and mentally familiar. He likened it to a snail retreating into its shell, or a spider crouching at the center of a web it had worked so hard to spin. "Am I taking refuge within my ivory tower?" he asked. "And is this tower strong enough to protect me from these torments?

"Last night was an eternity," he thought. "Time, time. My time, Thi's time, the time of electrons and mesons. Is the time of the physical sciences independent of the time of the human mind?" More than once Doan had pondered and talked with Tanh about the subject of time. They had discussed time in Einstein's Theory of Relativity, and Tanh had observed that time, space, and what we call physical phenomena have an intimate relationship with human perception. Tanh had said that only through the human mind do these acquire the forms and natures by which we usually know them.

Doan could almost totally agree with Tanh. Recent discoveries in subatomic physics had all but brought down the whole edifice of materialist physics, so that the very foundation of existence presumed since Democritus had lost its credibility. Scientists were unable to find anything that had a separate, independent existence. Whenever they conducted subatomic experiments, they were able to record only the entities' reactions, sometimes as waves, sometimes as particles. They could not locate a "self," only their own conceptions.

Doan knew that neither matter, space, nor time can be observed independently of the other two. He knew that a line between the past and the future, called the present, is normally assumed. But in his study of Relativity, he discovered that the span of the present varies with the distance in space between the observer and the phenomenon observed. The present might be a short span of time, but it can also be measured in years, or even tens of millions of years. Someone on the Earth watching a falling star may not know that from other points in the universe the star has not yet fallen, or it may have fallen millions of years before. The present is not a universal entity. It can also be identified with the past or the future.

Doan understood from quantum mechanics that there comes to be an infinite indeterminate with regard to speed and energy when one tries to specify the position of an electron. One cannot satisfactorily describe the actions and reactions of subatomic matter by mathematical formulas. In the domain of subatomic physics, the very nature of space and time becomes imprecise, so that one cannot always tell what is past and what is future. Some subatomic "entities" even seem to go in the opposite direction of time, in the reverse direction of the causal order itself.

Doan had the feeling he was moving from one dream to another. Thi had been a part of his world for almost eight years, and yet his son never seemed so real as he did now at the threshold of death. Doan could see Thi more clearly, thus he could see himself more clearly. His illusions of security and permanence had evaporated, and human life seemed as fragile and evanescent as a wisp of smoke. The past seemed like a dream. But what about the present, filled with anxiety and fear, was it not also a dream?

Doan became aware of a new yearning within him. He wanted to awaken from his illusory dream world and enter the world of reality. He realized that time and space were a net imprisoning him. Thi's critical condition, a source of overwhelming anxiety, had become a doorway to Doan's liberation. Through the ordeal of his son's illness, Doan had come to realize that his world of scientific re-

search was as valid as the world of everyday preoccupations.

For Doan, certain facts, perhaps amusing to
most people, were primordial truths to be deeply
contemplated. He would watch the bright red sun
setting over the mountain, its rays warming his
face, and realize that it had actually set eight minutes before—the sun one sees is never the sun of the
present moment. He would contemplate the star
that the poet speaks of "plucking from the firma-
ment to fasten to his beloved's hair" and he realized that it may have exploded millions of years
ago. His son Thi was born in 1972. "This fact
alone, seen from different points in the universe,
has different meanings," Doan thought. "From
some places, Thi has not yet been born. In other
locations in the universe, Thi will be very much
alive, laughing and talking, one thousand years
from now." By contemplating facts such as these,
Doan realized that most human beings live their
lives based on illusory perceptions which cause
them untold pain and fear.

Now he understood the practical implications
of knowing that electrons are manifestations of
waves and particles. What he saw, heard, and
touched every day were just so many phantoms. In
the light of science, the most common assumptions
about the solidity of things were proven erroneous.
Doan suddenly comprehended that his anxiety
about the possibility of Thi's death had been based
on illusory perceptions. This realization burst in
his mind like a flash of lightning.

Doan was totally aware of his son's critical
condition, but he was no longer in a panic. All

night, his state of mind had been too tumultuous to subdue or even to lull to sleep with pills. But his scientific understanding had come forward in a moment of need to offer him deep insight into the nature of existence. Scientific inquiry had proved to be his snail's shell and spider's web.

Doan sat at his desk, motionless and silent like a Taoist priest. If someone had asked him, "What is your innermost wish at this moment?" he would have answered, "To achieve total awakening." He did not wish to return to the dream of a son in perfect health and himself busily engaged in research and teaching. Although exhilarating, it was still a dream, and Doan knew that even beautiful dreams can be followed by nightmares, such as the one he had just lived through.

Instinctively, Doan caught hold of himself, and sat upright. He began to breathe slowly and deeply. Thoughts of birth and death arose. Doan knew that homo sapiens had derived from the single-celled creatures, and he smiled as he thought that life had been continuous from one little amoeba to himself. "Evolution is birth and death, but it is also non-birth and non-death. The amoeba has never died, and neither have I. When was I born? Didn't I exist even before the first amoeba, in the very conditions which had made the creation of the amoeba possible? I have never died from the very beginning, so how can I die now?" Once, Tanh had said to him, "Birth and death are like stars in your eyes," but Doan had not understood.

Now he remembered that the French chemist Lavoisier had said, "Nothing is created, nothing is destroyed." Doan thought that the Lavoisier rule, intended to describe inorganic matter and energy, could be applied to the domain of organic matter as well. All creatures endowed with life are also beyond birth and death. Doan's life and Thi's life would continue uninterrupted. They were beyond destruction. Although a drop of water may become a cloud, rain, or a grain of rice, the river of life flows uninterrupted. "Nothing is created, nothing is destroyed." "Nothing is born, nothing dies." How strange, Doan thought, that the language of science and the language of Buddhism are so similar.

Doan recalled the words of a philosopher, "I accept the limits imposed on my life in terms of space, so why shouldn't I accept the limits imposed by time? In the year 2000, only some of us alive now will still be alive, and none of us will be alive in the year 3000." Doan found this way of thinking mechanical and simplistic.

He knew that all phenomena are interdependent, that we are all part of the entire universe, and it is because we exist that other phenomena and the universe exist. "To live means to live with the entire universe," Doan thought. "Who can say that when I clap my hands, the sound will not, in some small way, disturb the entire Andromeda Constellation? Who can say that when I take a breath, the air that enters my lungs does not contain a tiny amount of air breathed by Julius Caesar centuries ago?

"To exist means to live in the totality of time with no beginning and no end. If there is no past, then there is no present or future. If there is no future, there is no present or past. Birth and death are conventional expressions, but they obscure the

vision of a total reality which has never been born
and will never die."

For over a year, Doan and Tanh had been having conversations on subjects like this, but suddenly Doan realized their real importance. "We are
bound by our perceptions," Tanh had said. "It is
our faculty of perception which divides reality into
birth and death, one and many, permanent and
impermanent, past and present."

Tanh had jokingly told Doan that his world of
elementary particles was a world of ghosts. Now
Doan understood that it was through this "world of
ghosts" that he was able to see through the illusory
nature of the ordinary world and grasp that the
things we perceive through our senses are themselves illusions.

Discoveries in physics during the past fifty
years have made it clear that things are not what
they seem. Though Doan and his colleagues were
all in agreement on this point, for almost twenty
years scientists had been debating issues such as
"wave and/or particle." Though hardly anyone
would dream of describing the subatomic world by
means of visual concepts, mutually contradictory
notions like "particle" and "wave" remained. The
scientist's perception was trapped within dualistic
vision, seeing reality in terms of pairs of opposites.
Although this vision had cracked with regard to
phenomena whose very natures seemed to be in
contradiction—matter and energy, inertia and
gravity, time and space, space and matter, wave
and particle—it remained intact concerning phenomena such as matter and spirit, subject and object. The arguments against a dualistic vision were

not yet strong or clear enough to bring about its total dissolution. Otherwise, how could scientists acknowledge the non-dualistic nature of time and space, and yet continue looking for the ultimate beginning and limit of the universe? The Big Bang Theory, the talk of a universe that expands, or has definable limits, seemed to deny the oft-stated conviction that time-space is a non-dualistic reality.

Recently Doan had heard a prominent scientist speculate about time inside black holes and within subatomic matter. Time and space were discussed as if they could be experienced locally, separate from subjective perception. The Theory of Relativity tells us that matter and space are of the same nature, and that time does not exist independently of space. Thus, all three phenomena—time, space, and matter—have the same nature. They do not exist outside of perception.

Some scientists have stated, "We can never know subatomic bodies unto themselves. We can only observe them through our own perceptions. As a result, any observation of the infinitesimal can only distort or change the observed object, and 'objective reality' remains unreachable." Doan realized that scientific observation is built on duality, that the objects of observation are regarded as independent of the subjects who observe.

Tanh had told him that in Buddhism, "observation" gives way to "penetration." When you "penetrate" reality, the distinction between subject and object dissolves. Herein, Doan thought, lies the biggest stumbling block of modern science. Doan differed with scientists who believe that the language of mathematics is a solution to this problem. Doan regarded mathematics as a language of abstraction, born of the human brain, one which expresses human perception rather than the world itself. However far we humans go, Doan pondered, we only come face to face with ourselves.

If only Tanh were here, he thought, Tanh could offer insight into "non-discriminative wisdom," the Buddhist method of seeing reality non-dualistically. Doan wondered what kind of language one might use when one reached that state. Obviously it would be one that did not divide reality into subjects and objects. In a sense, it would be an esoteric language because anyone who thought dualistically would find it difficult to understand a non-discriminative language. Perhaps notions conceived by Einstein such as "space-time continuum" and "four-dimensional space," or a notion conceived by nuclear physicists that a physical reality is at once "wave and particle," could be used to destroy the old dualistic notions of reality.

Yet, Tanh had also told him that in Buddhism, to destroy the dualistic vision does not mean to arrive at monism. If reality can be one, it can be two, or three. The Buddha would not say it is or it is not. Doan was ready to accept Tanh's explanation wholeheartedly. Truth must be found somewhere in a middle way.

Doan recalled some of Tanh's suggestions for ridding oneself of dualistic notions: "Buddhism offers concepts such as 'interbeing' and 'non-self' to break down the boundaries which divide reality." Doan thought, "Aren't Heisenberg's 'indeterminate relationships' also tools that could be used to wear down our habit of describing reality by those 'determinate representations'? Just as Buddhism has created its own language to help us go beyond dualism, science too has to create new language in order to express its new understanding of reality."

* * *

Doan stood up slowly. Through the window he could see the bright sun shining in the garden and dozens of birds rippling through the foliage. He yearned to go outside and stand among the strong, healthy trees. The worries and anxieties of the past night were still present, but he felt calm and full of energy. Doan's heart overflowed with tenderness as he thought of Tuyet and her struggle through this intense night and day. Doan shuddered at the thought that, in the terrible storm, he had been frail as a reed that could have snapped at any moment. He knew the pain of loss would be tremendous if Thi did not win his battle for life. But Doan had acquired a new strength and resilience which would help him withstand life's mishaps and give Tuyet support from then on. Like Tuyet and Tanh, he too possessed deep inner resources.

Doan reached the garden. The lily-like fragrance of the peony blossoms saturated the afternoon air. Doan was aware that for years he had been so absorbed in his world of neutrons, mesons, and electrons, that he rarely found time to hold his son's hand and walk with him. Now, having journeyed far into the world of subatomic physics, he was able to be truly present in this lovely, cool garden.

Doan walked towards the chestnut tree. The doorbell rang, and Tanh was standing at the gate. Doan walked slowly, very slowly, on the gravel path towards his brother-in-law.

Tanh watched Doan closely. He had never seen Doan walk that way before—with such composure, such majesty. Tanh whispered to himself, "Something wonderful has happened to Doan!" For a moment Tanh forgot that he too had had a marvelous breakthrough during the night.

The two men looked deeply at each other, seeing the entire universe and all eternity. In that moment, their love and gratitude for an eight-year-old boy, now lying in a nearby hospital at the edge of death, was expressed. Thi had shot an arrow, and it had struck two targets at the same time.

About the Author

Thich Nhat Hanh, born in 1926 in Central Vietnam, was the founder of the School of Youth for Social Service during the war. He was nominated by Martin Luther King, Jr. for the Nobel Peace Prize. Author of *Vietnam: Lotus in a Sea of Fire*, *The Cry of Vietnam*, *Being Peace*, and many other works, Nhat Hanh lives in exile in France, where he continues writing, teaching, gardening, and helping refugees worldwide.

About the Translators

Mobi Ho was born in Minneapolis in 1953. During the 1970s, she lived in Paris with the Vietnamese Buddhist Peace Delegation, helping Thich Nhat Hanh and Cao Ngoc Phuong work for Vietnamese people. She assisted on the South China Sea in a boat people rescue operation, and there she met her husband, Hoang Ho. Today they live in San Antonio, Texas, with their two children, and practice traditional Chinese medicine.

Vo-Dinh Mai was born in 1933 in Hue, Vietnam. An author, translator, and illustrator with more than twenty books to his credit, he studied at the Quoc-Hoc of Hue, and later at the Academie de la Grande Chaumière and the University of Paris. His paintings and woodblock prints have been exhibited in more than 50 solo shows and in numerous group shows in Asia, Europe, and North America. He lives and works in Maryland.